SIAMESE TALES OLD AND NEW

SIAMESE TALES OLD AND NEW

The Four Riddles and Other Stories

Translated by
Reginald le May, Ph. D. (Cantab), F. R. S. A.

*Late Adviser to the Siamese Government
in the Ministry of Commerce
and Communications*

With Some Reflections on the Tales

PILGRIMS

PILGRIMS PUBLISHING
◆ Varanasi ◆

Siamese Tales Old and New
Reginald le May

Published by:
PILGRIMS PUBLISHING

An imprint of:
PILGRIMS BOOK HOUSE
(Distributors in India)
B 27/98 A-8, Nawabganj Road
Durga Kund, Varanasi-221010, India
Tel: 91-542-2314059, 2314060, 2312456
Fax: 91-542-2312788, 2311612
E-mail: pilgrims@satyam.net.in
Website: www.pilgrimsbooks.com

Cover design by Asha Mishra

ISBN: 81-7769-681-5
ISBN: 978-81-7769-681-3

Printed in India at Pilgrim Press Pvt. Ltd. Lalpur Varanasi

CONTENTS

INTRODUCTION TO THE NEW EDITION

The art of storytelling is rapidly being lost, as modern electronic gadgets provide the 'new' world with processed entertainment at the press of a button. CD players, Televisions and the cinema have all but removed these practices from everyday life. It is even said that the television has killed the art of conversation thus leaving us with a vacuum that will be almost impossible to fill unless we try to revive some of the more traditional modes of story telling.

Thailand (Modern Siam) is no exception. Its rural communities, where such arts flourished, are being absorbed into the new race for modernity. In the headlong rush to the cities, the tales are in danger of falling into oblivion.

As a specialist in seeking out old titles for preservation, and in hoping to renew interest in lost arts, Pilgrims is pleased to republish this entertaining book of humorous and enchanting stories.

It was first published in 1958. The translator's original preface is comprehensive, for it amply explains the dilemmas and difficulties to overcome in translating such stories into a readable and entertaining format for today's modern reader.

South East Asia has a not dissimilar culture to that of India. The religions followed as well as the contacts through trade and migration has all led to the build up of this closeness.

The stories allow one to imbibe the hidden secrets of Siam a centre of art and culture throughout the times. They cover the whole gamut of situations imaginable and will provide entertainment for the whole family on those dark winter evenings when one tires of the television and wishes to go to bed with a good book or wish to put junior to sleep in the evening.

Christopher N Burchett
Varanasi March 2008

INTRODUCTION TO THE NEW EDITION

TRANSLATOR'S PREFACE

FOR a number of years past I have been searching in Siam for stories which would be at once diverting to the reader and illuminative of Siamese character and customs. Some time ago I was able to discover a number of fairy-tales, such as those from the North of Siam which I embodied in my book, *An Asian Arcady*, as well as other stories adapted from the Ramayana, the great Indian Epic, which has also found a spiritual home in this country in the form of the Ramakien. But it is only recently that I have come into the possession, through the kindness of a Siamese friend, of a small volume of Siamese tales that appear to me to fulfil the conditions which I have always kept in mind in my search.

The late Phya Manunet Banhān, formerly a Judge of the International Court in Bangkok, who edited the present volume, states in his preface that he has chosen stories of a varied character, some material, some spiritual in their nature, to suit all tastes. I have carefully examined all the stories given, and have chosen a number of the more material stories, together with one spiritual story which is of an unusual kind; and now present them in translation to the English-reading public. Three of these stories, although the language used is in no way coarse, are, to say the least, broad or, as the Editor says, 'spicily humorous', and would perhaps be more suitable for a Chaucerian age. Still, I must confess that I have enjoyed translating them myself, and if I can do so without serious damage to my own morals, why should I not give them to you, dear reader, whose morals are undoubtedly less susceptible to attack than mine?

In the translation which I have made of these, to me, fascinating stories, my chief aim has been to preserve their spirit and their setting, and any of my Siamese readers with a knowledge of both languages, who is conversant with the originals, will, I hope, be able to agree that the picture presented is on the whole a true one.

In one particular I must crave the reader's indulgence. If he does not find in every case virtue receiving its just reward or the happy ending to which he feels he is entitled, I would ask him to remember that I am only the poor scribe, and have no authority to alter by jot or tittle the dramatic sense of a Siamese tale. I myself have often asked my Siamese friends why in their stories the rascal so frequently comes out on top to the discomfiture of the hero, as for instance in "The Four Jolly Robbers"; and I am invariably met with the answer, "But isn't it very often true?"

The Siamese mind, then, is essentially realist, and thinks it better that the story should be true to life with its dangers revealed, rather than that they should be safely hidden under the cloak of idealism. The true test of the story will come with the question, "With whom does our sympathy lie at the end?"

REGINALD LE MAY

EDITOR'S FOREWORD

Translated from the Siamese by Reginald le May

IN collecting and editing this little volume of stories, I feel that I am rescuing from oblivion a number of tales which have been heard from the lips of story-tellers for generations past, tales with a point, tales with a moral adorning them, tales in fact which deserve to be remembered and carefully laid to heart.

As all wise men will agree, it should form part of our education to hear and read stories with admonitions and warnings encased in them, so that we may train and discipline our minds to such a degree as to know instinctively, as the occasion arises, how to conduct ourselves and regulate our actions in a suitable, orderly manner.

Some of these stories may, perhaps, have a spice of humour mixed with the morality, some perhaps with even more than their fair share of humour; but as long as the words used are not coarse and do not encroach on the realm of obscenity, no doubt this very humour and spiciness will invest them with an added zest.

I have, therefore, chosen stories which are likely to make a universal appeal, some of a more material, others of a more spiritual nature, and have collected them in this volume in the hope that they may be of some profit and amusement to the reader.

At the same time, it will be realized that the tellers of old fables and tales are, as a rule, by no means in a position to vouch for the truth of them, and I hope therefore that the reader will not add to my difficulties by making a point of diving into the substance of each story, or into the name of each individual, to ask himself, "Is this true or not?" In point of fact, if the truth be known, the desires of the teller and the reader are identical.

What they both seek are tales with a moral purpose salted with humour. In bringing these stories together, then, I have tried to bear these needs in mind, and, if I have failed, I must ask the reader to pardon me, whose sole aim is to instruct and entertain him.

PHYA MANUNET BANHĀN

SIAMESE TALES OLD AND NEW

i

THE FOUR RIDDLES

"An old slave and a loving wife—put not your trust in these."
OLD SIAMESE PROVERB

IN the golden days of long ago there was a youthful, handsome King who was inordinately fond of women, and spent almost all his hours in the company of his palace ladies. But this let it be said. It was not only their beauty of grace and form that held his senses in captivity and bound them with silken cords; these, indeed, he worshipped, as do all proper men. But he put all his trust in woman's good faith, and woe betide the evil tongue that so much as whispered one word against them in his presence!

Now it happened one day that, attended by a company of beautiful ladies, the King rode out to a forest not far distant from his capital, and while galloping along a path saw by chance a man and his comely young wife cutting firewood in a copse adjoining the glade. It occurred to him that it would be entertaining to inquire into the joys and sorrows of their lives, so he stopped the cavalcade and, dismounting near a shady tree, gave orders for the couple to be brought before him. When they arrived and had prostrated themselves before him, the King asked the husband what his means of livelihood was, to which the peasant replied that, as the court saw, he and his wife gained their simple living by cutting and selling firewood.

"And do you earn a sufficient living by this means?" asked the King.

"Yes, Your Majesty," replied the husband.

"And are you able to save any money?"

"A certain amount, Your Majesty."

"And what do you do with the money you save?"

At this the husband thought awhile, and then gave the following answer:

"Your Majesty, all the money I am able to save, after paying the expenses of our frugal household, I divide into four parts. The first part I bury in the ground; the second part I use to pay my creditors; the third part I fling into the river; and the fourth and last part I give to my enemy."

At this unexpected reply the King looked keenly at the man, who crouched motionless before him, and guessed at once that he was speaking in riddles, and excellent ones at that; so he ordered him to tell him the answers to the riddles, as he had a mind to use them. The husband agreed to do so, if the King would send his courtiers away, and when they had gone, he spoke as follows:

"The money I bury in the ground is the money I spend on alms and in making merit.

"The money I give to my creditors is what it costs me to keep my father and mother, to whom I owe everything that I have.

"The money I fling into the river is the money I spend on gambling and drink and opium; and

"The money I give to my enemy is the money I give to my wife."

Having written the answers down, the King read them carefully through, and then spoke to the husband thus:

"The first three answers please my mind, and I agree with them, but the fourth I condemn utterly, for I will not hear a word spoken against a woman. You are wrong to speak, or even to think, such evil thoughts."

Then he summoned the woman as well, and in her presence he spoke to the husband again:

"These four riddles must be kept secret—on no account tell the answers. If you breathe them to a living soul, I will have you arrested and shut up in prison for the rest of your life."

With these words the King left his seat beneath the tree and, gathering up the cavalcade, rode back to the capital, pondering on the strange riddles which had been given him by the woodcutter. Reaching the palace, he caused them to be inscribed on parchment scrolls, and issued a proclamation broadcast that whoever should guess the correct answers to all four riddles would be rewarded with a nugget of gold as large as a melon. For he wished to test the intelligence and minds of his people.

The months went by, and still no one could guess the answers to the riddles, until at length one day the royal messengers happened to pass in front of the woodman's house, and called out the King's proclamation. As soon as the wife heard it, she recognized at once that the riddles asked were those propounded by her husband. She knew, too, that her husband had given the answers to the King, and she thought within her heart:

"To-night I will ask my husband for the answers, and if he will give them to me, to-morrow I will go straight to the King and claim the reward of gold. If I can only get a nugget of gold as large as a melon, no longer need I share the hardships of wood-cutting with this miserable husband of mine. No. I'll hide the nugget in the ground and say nothing to him; and if the King inquires afterwards how I came to know the answers to the riddles, I shall speak the truth at once and say that my husband told me. Then the King will certainly have my husband arrested and put in prison for the rest of his life; but I shall be wealthy and able to find a new husband, much nicer than the poor creature I live with now."

With these thoughts in her mind, when her husband came home from work that evening, she told him what had happened, and begged him to tell her the answers, in order that she might claim the reward of gold. But he, fearing the royal wrath, would not tell her, and reminded her of the King's command. So she kept silent; but as soon as bedtime came, she pretended to cry and to sob bitterly; and when her husband asked her the cause, she refused to answer. Then the woodcutter's heart began to melt, for his wife was young and beautiful, and they had not long been married. So he took her in his arms and, embracing her, said, "What is the matter, sweetheart? Are you angry with me, or is there anything in the world you want me to do? However difficult it may be, I will try my utmost to do what you wish, only tell me what is troubling your mind."

This was her opportunity and, looking up at him, she said through her tears:

"All my love and gratitude is yours, my darling. Ever since we have been married I have worked with you and played with you, and shared your joys and sorrows, your troubles and hardships. You know that I regard myself as your child, and only look to our life together until the day we die. But it hurts me sorely that you cannot see into my heart and will not trust me. You will not even tell me the answers to your stupid riddles, as if we were not man and wife and true lovers. What sort of man can it be who will think such evil of his wife?"

Hearing his wife appeal to him to put his whole

trust in her, the husband's heart became as velvet and he believed her words, for he loved her dearly, and she fondled him as only a wife can. So he told her the answers that night, and they slept in each other's arms.

But when the morning came, and the woodman had taken a loving farewell of his wife and gone to his work, then off she sped to the capital and, entering the palace gate, told the officer on guard that she had come to answer the King's riddles. She was duly led into the King's presence and, as each riddle was put to her, she gave the correct answer just as her husband had told it. Then the King acclaimed her as the winner of the prize, and ordered that the nugget of gold should be given to her. But, as she was about to leave the palace, the King was fired by a sudden suspicion, and he ordered the woman to be brought again before him.

"Who are you? Have I not seen you somewhere before?" asked the King.

"Yes, Your Majesty, I am the woodcutter's wife," answered the woman.

"And how did you discover the answers to the riddles?"

"My husband told me them, Your Majesty," replied the wife.

At this the King frowned in anger, but he had given his royal word, so he dismissed the woman with her prize. Then he at once ordered guards to be sent out to arrest the husband and bring him to the palace. As the woodcutter lay bound before the King with guards on either side of him, the King questioned him, saying: "We warned you clearly of the punishment awaiting you if you gave to anyone the answers to the riddles. You knew you would be put in prison for life. Why did you tell them to your wife in defiance of the royal order, and thus bring down Our wrath upon you?"

The woodcutter at once acknowledged his fault and his disobedience to the King's command, but pleaded that he had done it because he loved his wife, and laid before the King all that had happened from the time when the royal messengers had read the proclamation by trumpet, and his wife had heard it outside their home. But the King was wroth and would not listen, and ordered the guards to take the woodcutter and cast him into prison, for he had disobeyed the royal command. As the guards stepped forward to seize him, the woodcutter gazed firmly at the King, and spoke as follows:

"Your Majesty, as I have said, the reason why I told my wife the answers to the riddles was because I loved her and trusted her. I believed that she would keep the secret even as I. But my wife has not acted faithfully towards me. She has betrayed me, and has thus borne out the answer to the fourth riddle with which Your Majesty would not agree. You will remember, 'The money I give to my enemy is the money I give to my wife.' What view does Your Majesty hold of it now?"

At the woodcutter's words the King's mind went back at once to the riddles, and he saw that all the answers were true, even as the man had said. So he was graciously pleased to pardon the woodcutter, and in place of punishment loaded him with fortune and honour in accordance with his due.

NOTE BY PHYA MANUNET BANHĀN.—This is a notable example of the dangers which a husband runs if he tells his secrets to his wife. As the ancient saying goes, "A male elephant, a cobra, an old slave, and a loving wife—put not your trust in these."

ii

THE TWO MOTHERS

"*If you don't hear the story clearly, don't carry it off with you under your arm.*"—SIAMESE PROVERB

A FEW years ago there wasa young Siamese named Nai Sut Chai living with his mother, who was a widow, in a floating house on the river Menam Chao Phya, just below Bangkok. In due season he took to himself a wife, named Nang Som Boon, who lived also with her widowed mother in Klong Bang Luang, a canal on the west bank of the river opposite to Bangkok. The two houses were distant from one another about an hour's journey by boat, but as a rule Nai Sut Chai always lived with his wife in her mother's house.

Now the two mothers were beginning to advance in years and were both reaching an age when ailments are not uncommon. It happened one day that a servant arrived at Nang Som Boon's house with a message to say that Nai Sut Chai's mother was ill. Knowing that his mother was growing old, Nai Sut Chai became rather alarmed and said to his wife: "I think I had better go and pay the old lady a visit, to see if I can be of any help. There's no knowing what may happen to her these days." Nang Som Boon agreed and said that she would like to go with him too, but as it happened her own mother was also ailing at the time and she felt she ought not to leave her alone. After talking the matter over, it was eventually agreed between them that Nang Som Boon should stay and look after her own mother, while Nai Sut Chai should go and see what was the matter with his.

So off he went, but, finding that his mother was only suffering from some migraine inseparable from old age, he stayed and comforted her for a few days until she was quite recovered, and was then thinking of returning home, when by chance his aged aunt, who lived close by his mother's floating house, suddenly fell seriously ill and died. As she had no male relations in the house, Nai Sut Chai felt it his duty to stay behind and make all the necessary preparations for the cremation of the body. But all the time he was thinking of his wife's mother, who he knew was also ill, and of whom he had had no news since he left his wife's house.

On the day following her mother's death, the aunt's daughter, having shaved her head and put on her white 'panung'[1] and 'pahom',[2] went off in her canoe and paddled up Klong Bang Luang to buy fruit and betel-nut for the ceremony of her mother's cremation. As she was approaching the house of Nang Som Boon, the latter, who happened to be outside on the verandah, saw the girl coming along dressed all in white with shaven head, and thought at once in her fearful heart: "The worst has happened. Nai Sut Chai's mother must be dead, or why should she dress in mourning? If I take no notice of her, and he comes back and finds that I know nothing about it, he will think I'm very hard-hearted; for, as a rule, if you love your husband, you must love his mother as if she were your own." With these thoughts in her mind, she called to the girl, and, with anxiety written all over her face, asked her: "How is the old lady, is she very ill?"

The girl naturally thought that Nang Som Boon was referring to her mother, and answered: "I am sorry to say that she's dead; she died yesterday. We are going to cremate the body to-morrow morning at the Temple." With this, being in a hurry, she pushed off from the steps of the house and gave Nang Som Boon no time to

[1] Lower garment. [2] Bodice.

obtain any further details which might have enlightened her as to the true state of affairs. So, although the old lady was really alive and well, Nang Som Boon was convinced that her husband's mother was dead, and, as her own mother had by this time recovered her health, very early on the following morning she got into her boat and went off down the Klong to take part in the cremation ceremony of Nai Sut Chai's mother.

In the meantime Nai Sut Chai had also shaved his head and clothed himself in white, and at the appointed time had superintended the transport of his aunt's body to the Temple. On his arrival he made the customary offerings and merit, but in his heart he was really thinking of his wife's mother and wondering whether she was still alive or dead too. So all the time he kept a keen watch on the boats in the Klong as they came in and out, to see if he could discover anyone who lived near his wife's house and could give him news of her mother. But, although he watched for a long time, he saw nobody he knew.

Now his wife, when she arrived near the Temple, moored her boat to the bank, and without being visible herself, stopped to watch the people in the Temple grounds to see what they were doing and how they were dressed, before she actually went to take part in the ceremony. As she watched, she saw Nai Sut Chai and all his relations dressed in white with shaven heads, preparing to place the body in the 'Sala' near the water's edge, and at once thought to herself, "I am dressed in white all right, but I have forgotten to shave my head." So she slipped quietly away again in her boat without being seen and paddled her way back till she came to a shop where she could get her hair shorn off. This being accomplished, back she went again to the Temple, and presently Nai Sut Chai, who was still watching out for someone from his wife's neighbourhood, suddenly saw his wife entering the Temple grounds with shaven head and dressed in white like the rest of them. His heart at once became as ice, for he felt certain in his mind that his wife's mother must be dead also, and he could only stand and gape. His wife, seeing him thus with sorrowful face and tearful eyes, ran at him with a cry of grief and embraced him. He on his part held her up and started to ask her, "Mother's dead, isn't she?" but he could only get as far as "Mother's dead", and the words of questioning stuck in his throat for sobs. This was too much for his wife, who clasped him round the neck and burst into tears. Thus they stood, embracing one another and sobbing as if their hearts would break, in front of the whole company of mourners. The mourners, in their turn, looked at one another in amazement and began to ask themselves what all this pother was about. As one said to another: "When Nai Sut Chai's old aunt died, he never uttered a single howl or shed a single tear. They can't be weeping over her death; there must be something else very serious that has taken place." They did not like to interrupt the pair, so they waited to see what would happen.

Nai Sut Chai and Nang Som Boon embraced one another so fervently and sobbed so loudly that they had no chance of speaking, but after they had remained thus for as long as a cheekful of betel-nut can be chewed, their tears and grief began to abate somewhat, and at last Nai Sut Chai, who got in the first word, was able to blurt out: "Oh dear, oh dear, ever since I left you I have been full of anxious frightened thoughts, but I never dreamt that she was so ill as to die like this."

To which Nang Som Boon replied: "Oh, I am so sorry that I didn't look after her myself. I shall never forgive myself for this, never."

This astonished Nai Sut Chai, who said: "But what do you mean, darling, weren't you there all the time—you never left her, did you? Why do you say that you didn't look after her?"

Still his wife entirely misunderstood the drift of his question and thought her husband was angry with her and was being sarcastic, because she hadn't visited his mother more often. So she began to cry again and fell on his neck once more, saying: "It's really true, I swear it's true; I had no idea the old lady was so desperately ill. I am really sorry to the bottom of my heart, and although I was not able to nurse her, yet I should not have minded so much if I had been with her on her death-bed."

These words of his wife only caused Nai Sut Chai more astonishment than ever, so he asked her again: "But surely, darling, you were actually in the house when she died, weren't you?"

This time it was Nang Som Boon's turn to be astonished, as she saw from his manner that her husband was not being sarcastic, but was really in earnest with his questions, so she replied: "No, how could I be? I only learnt the news when your aunt's daughter came by and told me that your mother was dead."

Then Nai Sut Chai realized that there must be some mistake somewhere, so he dried his tears and said: "But look here, darling, what are you talking about? Whose mother did you think was dead?"

"Why, yours, of course," answered she.

"Oh, that's all nonsense. My mother isn't dead. She's alive and quite recovered."

At this the well of Nang Som Boon's tears dried up as if by magic, and it was her turn to ask: "Well, if that is so, what are you crying and making all this fuss about?"

To which her husband replied: "I saw you coming into

the Temple all dressed in white, with shaven head and sobbing bitterly as you came, and I thought it was your mother who had died."

"Well, why are you dressed in mourning and whose is this body you are going to cremate?" asked Nang Som Boon.

"This is the body of my aunt, who died the day before yesterday. That's why I am in mourning," answered Nai Sut Chai. "But why did *you* shave your head and put on these clothes?"

"Well, yesterday your aunt's daughter came to my house dressed in white, and when I asked her how the old lady was getting on, she replied that she was dead. So I came down this morning, and when I saw you all at the Temple, I thought it was your mother who was being cremated, so I went and got shaved too."

At this Nai Sut Chai burst into laughter and said to his wife: "Of course, she thought you were referring to her mother, and so she replied truthfully that she was dead. But you thought it was my mother, and that's where you went wrong. And I thought it was your mother, and that's where I went wrong. What idiots we've been!"

As soon as they realized where they were, their grief disappeared, and in its place a feeling of shame stole over their faces as they thought of the exhibition they had been making in front of the whole company. And the company themselves, although they had assembled to take part in a cremation ceremony and sorrowful countenances were more fitting, still, when they thought of the scene which had just been enacted before their eyes could not repress their sense of humour. Some put their hands to their mouths and turned their heads away. Some laughed in silence until their sides and stomachs ached. And some actually had to flee outside the Temple's gates to give vent to their loud guffaws. And there we must leave them.

Note by Phya Manunet Banhān.—The moral of the story is this. If you listen to news carelessly, or believe news without making further inquiry, you are more often than not courting disaster. Remember the old proverb, "Rabbits are easily scared by noises", meaning to say, "They jump at conclusions". It's very applicable to the people in this tale.

iii

THE GHOULS' MARRIAGE

"*Man is padi, woman is rice.*"—OLD SIAMESE PROVERB

ABOUT a hundred years ago or more there lived in Rajaburi a young man named Nai Kaeo. His parents were honourable, well-to-do folk, but Nai Kaeo himself, by the time he was twenty-one, had gained an unenviable reputation among the townspeople as an idle young fellow, who, in company with his boon companions, spent his time in turning night into day and in exhausting the pleasures of the city. He took not the slightest care to educate himself, nor did he stir a finger to help his father in earning a livelihood; on the contrary, he preferred to spend his father's hard-earned money in entertaining the frail ladies of his acquaintance. His father and mother both upbraided him many times for his loose conduct, but he gave no heed to their words, for he was an obstinate, wilful young man, and had no respect for his parents' wishes. The fact is that he was an only son, and, as often happens in such cases, his father and mother had spoilt him and had allowed him to have his own way ever since he was a child.

One day it happened that Nai Kaeo was passing the garden of a wealthy family and saw the daughter of the house walking in it. The girl, whose name was Meh Pian, was just sixteen years of age, and had a very attractive form and face. Her demeanour was modest, and she was indeed a virtuous, diligent girl. As soon as he saw Meh Pian, Nai Kaeo fell violently in love with her; but as he did not know either her or any of her family, he could only use secret means to try and get into amorous intercourse with her, just as he had done so often before with other girls; but all his endeavours failed, for Meh Pian was a clever girl, who knew how to look after herself. She had always been obedient to her parents, and, although she soon knew of the passion that she had aroused in Nai Kaeo's heart, she never presented him with any opportunity to declare his love. However many go-betweens came to Meh Pian on Nai Kaeo's behalf, she gave them no encouragement whatever. Indeed, she scolded most of them for daring to approach her; but the go-betweens concealed the truth and brought back false statements to Nai Kaeo that Meh Pian returned his love and sent him many affectionate messages. They wanted, of course, to earn their hire, but it was not long before Nai Kaeo discovered that he was being deceived by the old women he was employing, and he tried to find other go-betweens to act on his behalf. Yet one and all deceived him just the same, and at the end he was no further advanced than at the beginning. Having failed of his own endeavours, and being at his wits' end, he had no other recourse but to turn to his father and mother for help. So he begged them to approach Meh Pian's parents and ask them to consent to their daughter becoming his wife. His father and mother thought it very unlikely that Meh Pian's parents would agree, for they knew well the reputation of their own son and that he could not compare with Meh Pian herself, but at the same time they feared that, if they did not bestir themselves on his behalf, Nai Kaeo would lose his self-control entirely and go from bad to worse. In the end they agreed to do so, and persuaded some of the elders of the town to go to Meh Pian's parents and ask them if they would consent to give Meh Pian to their son in marriage. But Meh Pian's father and mother very quickly found out what kind of a young man Nai Kaeo was, and after taking counsel with their friends, told the elders that Nai Kaeo was an idle rascal, who had never made any attempt to earn his living in accordance with his station in life. If they gave their daughter to him in marriage, it would only end in both of them being reduced to misery, and finally he would drag them, the parents, down too. As the old saying goes, "If you throw a snake away with your hand, be sure that it doesn't twist its tail round your neck." They therefore sent back word to Nai Kaeo's parents that they were sorry, but must definitely decline to give their daughter to him.

When these words were brought to Nai Kaeo's ears, it reduced him almost to despair, so sick was his heart from craving. But the more he despaired, the more violently in love he grew with Meh Pian, and he still sought in his mind for means to possess her. At last, when he was almost at the end of his resources, an opportunity offered itself to achieve his desire, and his star began to rise, a lucky star for him, but an evil one for Meh Pian.

It so happened that there was another young man in the neighbourhood named Nai Tong, who bore an excellent character for honesty and energy. The so-called pleasures of the town made no appeal to him, and he lived a quiet, sober life with his parents. They in their turn were anxious that he should marry and settle down as soon as possible, and knowing Meh Pian to be an attractive girl as well as a pattern of virtue, sent to ask for her hand for their son, Nai Tong. Meh Pian's parents were delighted at the offer and readily consented to the marriage; and, Meh Pian being herself agreeable, the wedding day was soon fixed.

When Nai Kaeo heard of this, as he very soon did, his heart became as jelly, and his last hopes, loosed from their moorings, went floating away to sea. It was, indeed, almost more than he could bear, and he loudly bewailed his unhappy fate to all his family and friends. Eating, sleeping, sitting, walking, his thoughts were ever on the same theme, and it seemed to him that all around him were eternally whispering in his ear, at every hour of the day and night, the date of Meh Pian's marriage with Nai Tong. In very truth his fears were only too well founded, for the fateful day drew ever nearer and nearer. On and on it came, with remorseless tread, with never a halt or backward step; and Nai Kaeo's heart began to burn within him, as if it were being consumed by fire. At times he thought he would enter the priesthood. At times a wild idea came into his head to go and kill his enemy, Nai Tong. At other times his only thought was to do away with himself and end his misery for good and all. His mind became such a turbulent, restless sea of thoughts that he could neither eat nor sleep. He found it impossible to stay at home, and spent his hours in wandering aimlessly about like a madman.

Now one day Nai Kaeo was passing the shop of an old woman who was a well-known barber in the town, when he happened to meet her at the door. Being an old gossip, she knew all about Nai Kaeo's troubles, but she appeared to be very surprised at his appearance and innocently asked him what was the matter, and why he looked so wild and downcast. Nai Kaeo unburdened his heart and told her the whole story, but, to his astonishment, the old woman only laughed and said: "You seem to be making a lot of fuss about nothing. I don't see anything to be so sad about. So you want Meh Pian as a wife, do you? Well, if that's your only trouble, young man, just leave it to me, and I'll easily fix that up."

At these reassuring words Nai Kaeo began to forget his troubles somewhat and to take heart again; and he promised the old woman that, if she actually succeeded in stopping the marriage of Nai Tong and Meh Pian and in obtaining Meh Pian as a wife for him, he would give her five 'chang'[1] in hard cash.

The old woman accepted the task cheerfully and guaranteed its success, saying: "Now, don't you say a word to anybody. Just go home and keep quiet, and don't be anxious. Leave it all to me, and I will arrange everything myself. When I have completed my share of the task, I will come and tell you, and then, when all is ready, it will be your turn to step in and claim your bride. You need not feel the slightest qualms—it will all be settled quite easily."

With this she dismissed Nai Kaeo and sent him back home. Then she gathered up her comb, mirror, scissors, razor, powder and oil, and made her preparations for the part she had to play as quickly as possible, for the wedding-day was approaching and there was no time to lose.

Now the old woman was known to almost every household, and was an especial favourite with the young girls, whom she used to visit to cut their hair and gossip. On the day of her conversation with Nai Kaeo she went straight to the house of a young lady, whom she knew to be a great friend of Meh Pian, and finding her at home, asked her whether she would like to have her hair cut. But without waiting for an answer, she sat down and began to engage the young lady in conversation after the manner of her kind, and they soon fell to gossiping about all the different people they knew. Very artfully she brought the talk gradually round to the subject of Meh Pian's marriage, and dropping her voice, said as if thinking aloud: "It really is rather a shame. Noo[2] Pian's father and mother are people of substance, and Noo Pian herself is such a pretty, charm-

[1] One 'chang' equals 80 ticals. [2] Noo is a term of endearment.

ing girl that I really feel very sorry for her. She has such nice manners and is so beloved of all, both young and old, that she deserves to have a very nice husband indeed. Don't you think so?"

Meh Pian's friend was very much taken aback and said to the old woman: "But what are you saying? Isn't Pian going to have a nice husband? What's the matter with Nai Tong? I think he's a very nice boy. He's very good looking; he's very steady, and will make a splendid husband for Pian. His parents are well off, and I can't see any possible objection. What do you mean by saying you're sorry for her?"

The old woman pretended to be astonished in her turn, and said with rather a cynical grin: "What do *you* mean? I never said anything about Nai Tong. Of course he is a nice boy. If he wasn't, would he be going to marry Noo Pian?"

The girl saw from the old woman's manner and the inflexion of her voice that she was speaking with sarcasm, and that there was some hidden meaning in her words, so she sidled up to her, and pressing her knees in a coaxing manner questioned her closely: "I see you know something—do tell it me and let me into the secret too. I promise I won't tell anybody."

But the old woman shook her head knowingly and said: "No, it's none of our business. You know the old saying, 'To know and tell is worth two pair of cowries, but to know and keep silent is worth a tamleung of gold'. It's far better still to know nothing at all. If it should get to the ears of Noo Pian, she will only be angry and come and tear out my grey hairs. I am an old woman now, and, if I go about gossiping and lay myself open to a young girl's tongue, I shall be covered with shame. If Noo Pian were related to me in any way, I could not bring myself to keep silent, because it's actually a very unpleasant affair. The more I think of it, the more sympathy I feel with Noo Pian, because, after all, she is a woman like myself. In the old days there was a common saying that 'Man is padi, woman is rice'. The nature of rice is that it can only be consumed. It cannot be planted like padi. If you are born a woman, how many husbands can you have? Whether he turns out good or bad, you have to put up with the first you get. You are not like a cup which, though defiled, you can clean again."

Hearing the old woman talk in this strange manner, the young girl thought to herself that Nai Tong must have something terribly wrong with him, which made her want to hear the story about him all the more; for it is a general rule that the more you make a secret of something, the more avid and curious other people are to know what it is. So she begged and implored the old woman to tell her the story, and finally, after much hesitation, the latter yielded to her entreaties. But before she began the old barber enjoined upon her the strictest secrecy and said: "If I tell you now, you must not breathe a word about it. If it should get to the ears of Noo Pian or her father and mother, they are sure to break off the marriage at once. So if you value Noo Pian's happiness, you won't mention a word about it to a living soul."

By this time the young girl's curiosity was so aroused that she was willing to promise anything, and she solemnly swore to the old woman that she would keep her secret inviolate, and would not tell a single soul.

Then the old woman bent her head and, sinking her voice to a whisper, said: "This young man, Aw [1] Tong, is a ghoul. I have known it ever since he was a child. His father and mother know it too, but they have kept it hidden from the world. Now I have told you this dreadful

[1] 'Aw' and 'Ee' are prefixes applied to ghouls, male and female.

secret, but, as you love me and Meh Pian too, do not repeat it."

With that the old woman gathered up her barber's tackle and, putting her basket under her arm, hurriedly left the house. When she knew she was safely out of sight, she went straight to the house of one of Nai Tong's friends, and, finding him at home, and knowing herself to be welcome, she sat down and asked for some water and betel-nut. While it was being brought she began to chat with Nai Tong's friend in a general kind of way, but all the time she was feeling her way round to the subject of marriage. When she saw the chance of an opening, she began in this wise: "Young Tong was born in this town, and I can't understand how he can be so foolish, but honestly I feel very sorry for him. He's a good fellow and a hard worker. He stays at home and doesn't go wandering about the streets, wasting his time with idle friends. So he doesn't know, of course, which girls are good and which girls are bad. He deserves to have a good wife, but you can't put the whole blame on him. It's really the fault of the old people, because it is they who have chosen his wife for him."

Nai Tong's friend listened to the old woman, half curious, half astonished, as he gathered from her words that Nai Tong was somehow or other going to get a bad wife. He naturally became rather alarmed in his mind, because he knew that Nai Tong was going to marry Meh Pian. It was clear to him that the old woman must know something very serious to the detriment of Meh Pian, so he looked at her searchingly and said: "You know, I suppose, that Nai Tong is going to marry Meh Pian? What do you mean by saying that she will make him a bad wife? Do you know anything about her which you ought to tell us?"

At this direct question the old woman appeared to be

startled, and, looking first to the right and then to the left, said in a frightened voice: "Heavens, you simply mustn't mention her name. When I spoke just now, I had no intention whatever of attacking Noo Pian. I was simply sorry for poor Tong, that's all. You remember the old saying: 'Once you have built your house, you have to live in it, for good or ill, until it falls down.' So once you've got your wife, you have to put up with her until she dies. Tong has never had a wife before, and is such an innocent boy that we ought to find him a thoroughly good wife for him."

Nai Tong's friend saw from the old woman's equivocal manner that she was concealing the truth, and became all the more curious to know what she had at the back of her mind. The more he thought about it, the more obscure her meaning became. In the whole district he had never heard an evil word spoken of Meh Pian, or anyone bring the slightest accusation against her. All the things he had ever heard said were entirely in her favour. He felt then he must follow the matter up and find out the true facts of the case. So he spoke rather severely to the old woman, and told her that, having gone so far, she must tell him exactly what she knew.

The old woman appeared to hesitate a great deal, but finally said that she would agree to tell him if he solemnly promised that he would not repeat it to anybody else, because she was afraid of its getting to the ears of the parties concerned.

Nai Tong's friend promised faithfully that he would keep her secret; whereupon she went up to him and whispered in his ear, "Ee Pian is a ghoul, and has been so ever since she was a child. Every night she creeps out and goes about her horrible, ghastly business. You just wait and see. I don't mind predicting that, if Tong marries Ee Pian, within three months she will have plucked out his liver and eaten it. Now I have told you the truth as you asked me, but if you have any regard for me, don't breathe a word about it to any other soul. Tong and Ee Pian have agreed to take one another as husband and wife, and the marriage day has already been fixed. Are we going to interfere now? After all, we are not related to them in any way. Surely it's better for all concerned if we say nothing."

With these words the old woman rose up abruptly and left the house.

The wise old woman knew what she was doing, and the value of such promises as her listeners had given to her. No sooner had she gone back home than Meh Pian's girl friend and Nai Tong's man friend rushed off to the respective families and related the story which each had heard from the barber's lips.

We can imagine the consternation which the stories caused, and the endless whisperings and consultations between the members of each family. And yet neither side dared to speak of it abroad, for they had no certainty of the truth of the stories. They were only rumours after all. The ones who suffered most of all were the unfortunate young couple on the eve of marriage, and poor Noo Pian, as soon as she heard the terrible news, shut herself up in her room and sobbed her little heart out.

As for the old woman, when she got back home she felt certain in her own mind that on the morrow both sides would send emissaries to her to find out the truth of the matter. At first she thought it might cause trouble if they both arrived together, but afterwards she said to herself: "It doesn't matter, after all, because if they do, neither party will mention the affair." Hardly had she had time, however, on the following day to consider the question, than Meh Pian's aunt arrived. She saw her coming in at the front door and tried to run out at the back, but the aunt was too quick for her, and cried out to her to stop. So she came back and said to the old lady rather brusquely: "What have you come here for?" The aunt was too distressed to make a long story of it, and inclining her head towards the old woman, said: "Is it true that Nai Tong is a ghoul? If you love us, let us know the truth, one way or the other."

The old woman pretended to be very angry on hearing that Meh Pian's friend had revealed her secret, but finally heaved a great sigh and said: "I see I can't disguise it any longer. It is true that Nai Tong is a ghoul, and has a tail. But even he himself doesn't know this, for he only goes out at night when he is fast asleep. Whenever he goes on his horrible errand, his tail comes out as long as your hand, but as soon as he gets back home and goes to sleep again, the tail disappears."

The aunt listened horror-struck and said: "What on earth are we to do? Both sides have fixed the marriage day, and it will be here very soon."

The old woman appeared to consider this in her mind, and after a time advised her to do nothing. "We can't very well stop the marriage now—we have no actual reason that we can give publicly. We can't calmly say that Nai Tong is a ghoul. We have no evidence to prove it, and it would only cause a dreadful scandal. The best thing to do is to let them be married, and then advise Noo Pian to watch out and catch him the very first night. She can easily pretend to be tired and go to sleep, and then, when she is certain that Nai Tong is asleep, she can grasp hold of his tail and pull it until he howls for mercy. The nature of a ghoul is such that, once it is caught, it is very ashamed, and Nai Tong of his own volition will refuse to live any more with Noo Pian as his wife. In this way the matter will be quickly settled, and they will be separated."

After turning it over, the aunt was, on the whole, satisfied with this idea, and when she returned home was able to convince Meh Pian and her parents that this was the best course to follow.

The following morning Nai Tong and his friend paid a visit to the barber. The old woman, after pretending to be extremely angry with the friend, allowed herself to be over-persuaded in the same way as before, and admitted to Nai Tong that Ee Pian was a ghoul who ate other people's livers by night. "You'll soon find out for yourself," she said, and added: "You wait until one night you go to sleep before Ee Pian, and you will find that she'll be after you quick enough."

At this Nai Tong cried out: "Good Heavens, if this is true, I'm not going to marry the girl. I'll break it off at once."

But the old woman jumped up and said: "No, no, you can't do that. How are you going to break it off? You can only go and say to her parents, 'Noo Pian is a ghoul, I won't marry her.' What proof have you got? I know you, you'll just say that I told you, and they'll all come down on me. But frankly I won't have it. I do you a good turn by telling you the truth, and then I get all the blame from the other side. No, no, this is not a trifling affair; it's serious, and that's why I did not want to tell anybody. This friend of yours forced me to tell him the secret, and now he has betrayed me."

With this she turned a face of wrath upon the wretched friend, who humbly begged her pardon. Then Nai Tong, who believed her implicitly, said: "Well, what do you advise me to do?"

To this the old woman slyly replied: "This is what you have to do. You can catch her quite easily. When you both go to bed, pretend that you are drunk and that you have fallen asleep. But keep on the watch and don't lose yourself for a moment. As soon as Noo Pian thinks you are asleep, she will attack you, but you must not let her actually get hold of you, for if she succeeds in doing so, even if you don't die, you'll become a ghoul too, and have to follow her through life. But if you can seize her hand before she actually touches you and squeeze it until she cries out, her parents will come running in, and you will have them as witnesses of what I tell you now. The nature of this kind of ghoul is such that, once it's caught, it is covered with shame, and Noo Pian will refuse to live with you any more."

Nai Tong agreed to follow the old woman's advice, and went back home with his friend. From that time, although neither party spoke a word of suspicion to the other, the relations between Noo Pian and Nai Tong became very strained, and it seemed almost as if they had suddenly grown to hate one another. At last the families ceased to pay visits, and prayed for something to happen to prevent the marriage.

The days went slowly by, and finally only two days remained before the marriage was to take place. Nai Kaeo, of course, knew nothing of what the old woman had planned, and came round to see her in a woeful state of mind. But the old barber cheered him up and laughingly said: "You go back home and keep quietly to yourself; don't go playing about or talking to others. Just wait till the day of the marriage, and then you'll find out what's going to happen."

These last words startled Nai Kaeo almost out of his mind, and he cried: "What, wait till the day of the marriage? Suppose there's a slip somewhere, I shall be done for. No, I can't do that."

But the old woman said: "Don't get alarmed. You are not going to get what you want at the time of the marriage. Your time's coming when Meh Pian is actually given to Nai Tong in the bridal chamber."

This only upset Nai Kaeo all the more, and he burst out: "But that's worse than ever. What are you talking about? Once Noo Pian and Nai Tong are in the bridal chamber together, there's no power, not even the angels, can help me then. If that's all you can do, I'll say good-bye, for you are of no use to me." His face darkened as he rose, and he thought to himself: "This cursed old woman is deceiving me like all the rest. There's only one thing left for me to do. I must go and kill Nai Tong."

But as he turned to go, the old woman's cackle of laughter brought him back to her side again. When he had seated himself on the floor, she unfolded to him the full story of what she had done, and had the satisfaction of seeing the colour come back to his face and the light to his eyes. In the end he was forced to laugh himself and to ask her pardon for having doubted her word. Then, thanking her for the help she was giving him, he went back to his own home.

Eventually the fateful day dawned. The parents and relatives of both parties set about their duties with seemingly open faces, but with secretly anxious, heavy hearts. Still neither side could draw back now, and finally both parties gathered together at the bride's house for the marriage.

The ceremony over, the parents of Meh Pian took her by the hand, it being by now evening time, and led her into the bridal chamber, where Nai Tong awaited her, and shut the door upon them. But when Meh Pian and Nai Tong found themselves face to face alone, they could not bring or trust themselves to speak, and such hatred was there in their hearts that they could not even look one another in the face. The only thought in the mind of each was how to catch the other tripping.

Meh Pian sat down on the floor with her head bent, and, with her arms round her knees, kept an awful silence.

Nai Tong at once said to himself: "This girl *must be* a ghoul, that's certain," for the old woman had told him that one of the characteristics of a female ghoul was that she was so ashamed that she could not speak or look one in the face. The more he thought about it, the more frightened he became, and the more he hated the sight of Meh Pian; but there was no present means of escape, and he must carry out his part of the drama, if he was to escape at all. So he pretended to be drunk and flung himself on the bed as if in a stupor, turning his face away from Meh Pian. As soon as she saw him fling himself on the bed, Meh Pian's heart went all of a flutter, for she realized that the time was soon coming for her to act, if she was to escape from the ghoul's clutches. With trembling heart she lay down on the bed with her back towards Nai Tong, and pretended to go to sleep. There they lay, each waiting with closed eyes but straining ears for the next move in the game.

Soon Nai Tong began to snore and murmur like a drunken man, giving every appearance of being in a heavy sleep. Meh Pian, who was straining every nerve, and whose heart was almost at bursting-point, hearing Nai Tong's louder and louder snores, thought to herself that he must be asleep at last, and turned round towards him so that she could watch his actions more closely. As she did so, although in an extremity of terror, she pushed out her hand ready to grasp Nai Tong's tail as soon as it appeared. But Nai Tong was also anxiously on the alert, and at once became aware that Meh Pian's hand was approaching him. He could scarcely breathe for fright, for he felt sure she was going to attack him. We can picture the terror of them both, with Meh Pian waiting to grasp the tail of Nai Tong, and Nai Tong waiting to grasp the hand of Meh Pian.

Meh Pian intended to approach Naí Tong as gently as she possibly could, but she shook so much with fear and excitement that suddenly she shot out her hand and struck the back of Nai Tong a sharp blow. This was more than Nai Tong could stand. Turning quickly round, he seized hold of Meh Pian's wrist and held it as if in a vice, crying out at the top of his voice: "Hi, hi, hi, I've caught the ghoul!" Now, although Meh Pian was as terror-struck as it is possible for a young girl to be, still, seeing Nai Tong behave exactly as the old woman had foretold, she overcame her terror for the moment, and in her turn screamed out: "Nai Tong's a ghoul, Nai Tong's a ghoul! Father, Mother, come quickly!" Hearing the screams and shouts, and fearing the worst, their parents and friends, who were all waiting outside, came rushing in, each party determined to save its own child, if possible. But when they found that each accused the other vehemently of being a ghoul, and that neither side was willing to listen to reason, the elders who had arranged the marriage managed to separate the shaking couple, and taking the parents aside, made it clear to them that, whatever they believed or thought, one thing was certain, Nai Tong and Meh Pian could not possibly remain together as husband and wife. And when the excitement and noise had subsided, and each party had had time to think the matter over, the parents on both sides agreed that the best thing to do was to return the marriage portion which each family had provided and dissolve the marriage then and there.

The next day the news spread like wildfire through the town of the scandal that had taken place, but Nai Kaeo had been waiting up all night in the vicinity of Meh Pian's house and had heard all that was going on.

When evening came, he took the five 'chang' he had promised the old woman and handed them over to her with a glad and grateful heart. The old woman received the money gracefully and said to him: "I have done my part. Now it is for you to do yours. But don't be afraid, no one will ask for Meh Pian's hand. Only wait a little while for the noise to subside."

And so it turned out in the event. The whole town heard and believed that Meh Pian was a ghoul and shunned her like the plague. No one came forward with any offer for her hand, and in due course Nai Kaeo, who had bided his time, sent his parents to ask again if Meh Pian was willing to have him for her husband. Meh Pian's parents took counsel together, saying: "Our child has lost her reputation and is likely to find no husband at all. This young fellow, Nai Kaeo, has been in love with Pian for many years now. Let us give her to him and make the best of a bad business."

So in the end Nai Kaeo achieved his desire and married Meh Pian after all, but of their life together the chronicles are silent, perhaps wisely. In any case, it is their affair, not ours.

iv

THE SNARE

"Three days' absence from your wife, and her heart is another's."
OLD SIAMESE PROVERB

SOME years ago there lived in Lopburi, hard by the old Palace wall, a couple who had been married some four or five years. The husband was a man of forty-five, but the wife was still a comely young woman of twenty-four, and, as sometimes happens in such marriages, she presently began to tire of the addresses of her middle-aged spouse, and to look round for a more ardent lover, nearer to her own age and liking. Nor was it long before she was successful in her search.

Now this couple kept an open shop which fronted the road to the market, the house itself standing a little way back in a garden. And as the husband was a stout, lazy fellow who loved his bed, on the nights when her lover came to visit her, which was pretty often, she used to lie awake until her husband was fast asleep and snoring, and then softly glide down from the house and slip gently into the arms of her lover, who was waiting for her in the shop. The boards were hard, but glowing love takes little heed of boards.

It happened one night, when so they lay in one another's arms, that sleep, which drives away all fear, overcame them. Unfortunately, that same night the father of the husband, who lived close by and who was now advanced in years, found sleep impossible, and at length rose up and went out into the road to take the air. As he walked slowly along, leaning on his stick, he passed by the open shop, and was astonished to see two human forms lying on the floor some little way inside. Shedding his heel-less slippers, with stealthy, soundless steps he crept towards the sleeping couple, and, bending down to examine their faces, recognized at once the form of his daughter-in-law lying in the arms of a man who was certainly not his son. "Ah!" said he to himself, "so my daughter-in-law has taken a lover, has she? I have long suspected this from her manner towards my son, and now it is sure beyond all doubt." Shaking his finger at the sleeping girl, he murmured: "Little wanton creature, take heed. To-morrow I shall tell your husband, and you will be beaten sore." And then to himself: "But it is no use my telling him in words alone, for a woman is far too clever not to outwit me there. I must take some tangible evidence of her misdoing."

As softly as he could, he leant down to remove a bracelet from her wrist; but even so he was not quick or gentle enough, for at the very moment that he touched her arm his daughter-in-law awoke, and realized that something was happening; and although she could not see the robber clearly, she was conscious that it was an elderly man, and guessed that it must be her father-in-law. So she made no sign or sound, but pretended to be fast asleep, for to her swift, feminine mind an idea had already occurred of how to escape the old gentleman's snare.

As soon as her father-in-law had taken the bracelet and was gone, she woke up her lover and sent him off in exactly the opposite direction, and then she herself glided back to the house and lay down by her husband's side once more. But a short while after, as he still lay peacefully snoring, she woke him up and said in a tired voice: "It's dreadfully hot in the house to-night. I cannot sleep at all. Let us go out into the open shop, it will be much cooler there." Her husband replied that he himself could sleep very well, but presently, seeing his wife's distress, and not wishing her to go alone, at length agreed to accompany her, and they both rose and went down into the shop. It was not long before the husband was fast asleep again, but the wife kept careful vigil, and at the end of a long and anxious hour woke him up again suddenly, as if in a state of great agitation, and cried: "Get up quickly. While we have been asleep a thief has been in and stolen my bracelet. What shall we do? It's no use trying to follow him now in the middle of the night. But we can't stay here any longer, let us go back into the house. I am sorry now that I suggested the idea." So back they went into the house again, the husband, simple, sleepy wretch, suspecting nothing.

On the following morning, as the husband was just finishing his meal, his father arrived, and, after the usual greeting, took him aside and said: "I have something very serious to tell you. Your wife is betraying you and has taken a lover. I found it out by chance last night. While taking a walk at a very late hour, I happened to pass by the front of your shop, and there I saw your wife in the arms of a strange man. I examined them closely, and I recognized her at once, but it certainly was not you who were with her. But I don't want you to trust to my words alone. I have brought this bracelet with me which I took myself from her wrist last night. Look at it, and you will recognize it as one that you gave her yourself." So saying, he handed the bracelet to his son.

But his son just laughed a happy laugh and replied: "Dear father, it is kind of you to take so much care for me and my honour, but I am glad to think that this time you have made a mistake. It was no lover that you saw with my wife in the shop, but I myself. My wife found it so hot in the house last night, that she persuaded me to go and sleep in the front of the shop. We were both fast asleep there when you came and took the bracelet from her wrist. She woke me up and told me that someone had taken her bracelet, but, of course, she thought, and I too, that it was a thief who had stolen it. How happy I am to think that it was just you, and that the bracelet is not lost after all. She was very upset about its loss, because she knew it was a present from me."

The old man, on hearing this, could scarcely contain himself for anger, both at his son's credulity and the wife's duplicity, and cried out: "You foolish fellow, it is not so. It's not true, my boy. I examined the man face to face, and I am sure it was not you. I should recognize him whenever I saw him again, although I do not know his name and have never seen him before. Do you think I am talking nonsense?"

But the son laughed all the more and said: "No, dear father, I am certain that you mean what you say, but you know that the shop must have been very dark, and, after all, you're an old man now, and your eyes are not what they were. Of course, I know that your intention is good, but honestly you must be mistaken, for it was I myself and not a lover. How could it be otherwise? *I know I was there!*"

The old man began to argue again, but the more vehement he became, the less his son believed him, and finally, when he saw that he was not making the slightest impression upon his son, he gave up the unequal task and sorrowfully hied himself home.

But the wife heard all that passed between them, and at their next meeting she and her lover laughed heartily at the success of her trick.

NOTE BY PHYA MANUNET BANHĀN.—The moral of this little story is that, whatever the matter may be, if someone whom we respect has an opinion opposite to our own, we ought not to dismiss it lightly, but turn it over and examine it fully. If we obstinately stick to our own opinions, refusing to listen to others or to budge one single inch, and maintain that "a rabbit has three legs," it will probably fall out to our own loss. So, even though we believe that we know the truth of the matter, if someone else offers us an opinion directly opposed to our own, we should weigh it carefully and draw therefrom what profit we can.

V

THE GLASS STOPPER

"When Greed comes in at one door, Fortune often goes out at the other."
OLD SIAMESE PROVERB

NOT long ago there lived in Bangkok a man of standing and rank named Phra Chamnān, who was well known as a dealer in gems. He was eagerly sought after by the Princes and nobles, and even more by their wives, for the selection and purchase of jewels, and his reputation as an appraiser of precious stones was such that you could not find his equal anywhere, search where you would.

There was also a fellow of no education or substance named Nai Kroh Dee, who, though of the lower orders, was yet on intimate terms with the dealer in gems, and visited him frequently. Now Kroh Dee had found by chance a small glass stopper which was broken at the base. Even so, it was a piece of well-cut crystal about the size of a berry, with a good water, and when the base had been ground down so as to remove all traces of the damage, and all the corners made sharp so that it had no similarity to a stopper, it certainly had, to the eye of a casual observer, the appearance of a large well-cut diamond. This stopper, well wrapped in cloth, Kroh Dee took to Phra Chamnān one day and said, "I have brought with me to show you a very ancient diamond, which has been carefully treasured in my family for generations. Now my mother has died and left me this gem as my share of the inheritance. But frankly I do not know what to do with it. It is far too big and too fine in quality for me to wear. Yet it's no use me keeping it stored away, and besides I am a poor man, and must needs have money to maintain myself. And so I have brought this valuable stone to you, and would ask you to be kind enough to sell it for me if you can. I do not ask you to buy it yourself, but you are a well-known dealer, so just let me deposit it with you, and if you get an opportunity, please do your best to sell it for me."

So saying, he very carefully undid the wrappings of cloth and handed the 'gem' to Phra Chamnān to see. When he saw it, Phra Chamnān laughed aloud, and, looking hard at Kroh Dee, replied: "What do you mean, you rascal, by bringing me a bottle-stopper and calling it a beautiful gem!"

This accusation upset Kroh Dee, who denied that it was a stopper, and affirmed stoutly that it was a very ancient jewel.

"It has been in the possession of my grandmother and great-grandmother, and has always been looked upon as a most valuable heirloom; but anyhow, even if you don't believe me, please take it and sell it if you can. I don't ask you to buy it, so you can think of it what you like."

Kroh Dee seemed so serious, and so affected by the doubts raised as to the genuineness of his stone, that Phra Chamnān agreed to receive it on deposit, and asked him how much he wished to sell it for. But when Kroh Dee replied that he wanted ten 'chang',[1] Phra Chamnān could not help bursting into laughter again and said shortly: "If you were to value it at a fuang,[2] perhaps somebody might buy it to tie round the cat's neck. Still, never mind, it's of no particular importance any way. I won't guarantee to sell it for you, but you can leave it with me, and if anyone happens to fancy it, I will see what I can do for you."

[1] One 'chang' = 80 ticals.

[2] One 'fuang' = $\frac{1}{8}$ tical.

Thereupon Kroh Dee left the 'jewel' with Phra Chamnān, and went out of the shop.

Three months went by, and Phra Chamnān had almost forgotten the existence of the 'jewel', when one day a Lao from the North came to visit him. The Lao told Phra Chamnān that he had been specially commissioned by the Prince of his State to purchase a diamond of the first quality to be set as a pendant to a necklace which the Prince wished to give to his principal wife. He had heard that Phra Chamnān was the most important gem-dealer in Bangkok, and so he had naturally come to him first. Would he be good enough to show him what he had in the way of diamonds?

Phra Chamnān brought out all his finest diamonds for the Lao to examine, none of which was as large as the stopper belonging to Kroh Dee. The Lao looked at them all very carefully, admired some and criticized others. If the water was good, the gem was too small; or, if the gem was the right size, then the water was poor. He could find none to satisfy him, and at length asked Phra Chamnān if he had no others, especially larger stones, to show him. By this time the latter was beginning to chafe at all his best stones being criticized in this off-hand manner, and, besides, he had no larger ones in stock; so he suddenly thought of the glass stopper that Kroh Dee had left with him. At first he felt too ashamed to bring it out, for it went hard against the grain of the first gem-dealer in Bangkok to say that a piece of cut crystal was a real diamond, but still he had no finer stones to show the Lao, and he had begun to realize that the latter had no real knowledge of precious stones. So he brought out the stopper in a nonchalant kind of way and, with every appearance of excuse, said: "As you don't seem to like any of my stones, perhaps you would care to look at this. It is not mine, and I don't guarantee it, but it has been deposited with me for sale, and possibly it may suit you."

No sooner had the Lao picked up the stopper and examined it, than he turned to Phra Chamnān and said: "This is just what I am looking for. The size is exactly right and the water is good. If the price is reasonable, my business ends here. How much do you want for it?"

Then the gem merchant thought rapidly to himself: "It's true that Kroh Dee only wants ten 'chang' for it, but if I ask only ten 'chang' for a fine diamond of this size, the Lao may have his suspicions. I'd better not do that. Twenty 'chang' would be nearer the mark, if the stone were a genuine one, and that would give me a profit of ten 'chang' for myself. Anyhow, the man's a fool, and will probably pay what I ask."

So, after a moment's reflection, he turned to the Lao and said briefly: "The owner is demanding twenty 'chang' "; to which the Lao replied that the price was a very reasonable one, and that he would conclude the deal there and then. "Unfortunately," he continued, "I have not brought so much money with me; I have only five 'chang' upon me at this moment. But I'll tell you what I'll do. I'll deposit these five 'chang' with you now, and I'll bring the remainder within seven days. Then you can hand over the jewel. But before I go, if you have no objection, I would like to put the matter on a business footing, and sign a short agreement to this effect. If I do not return and pay the balance in seven days, then you may confiscate this five 'chang' which I deposit now; but if I do bring the remaining fifteen 'chang', and for any reason at all you cannot hand me the jewel, then you must not only return me my deposit, but pay me a fine of five 'chang' as well. You may not attach much importance to it, but I am not buying this gem for myself, and the contract will be a guarantee of good faith on both sides."

Phra Chamnān was inwardly highly amused and said: "You need not be afraid of me; I shall not sell the jewel to anybody else."

"I dare say not," said the Lao; "but all the same, I have to cover myself, and, unless you strongly object, I would like to make this contract now."

So the agreement was made and duly signed and witnessed, and the Lao took his leave of Phra Chamnān.

Two days after this incident Kroh Dee was passing Phra Chamnān's shop, and, happening to find him at home, strolled in and said: "By the way, you remember that jewel I left with you some months ago to sell. Well, if you have not sold it already, I think I will take it back. I don't know where he comes from, but I hear there is a Lao in the town who is looking for fine diamonds, and it is quite possible that he might buy it from me. Have you been able to do anything with it?"

Now this simple request of Kroh Dee's placed Phra Chamnān on the horns of a great dilemma.

If he told the truth and said that he had already sold it to the Lao, Kroh Dee would quickly find out that the latter was paying twenty 'chang' for it, and would claim its full value, especially as he himself had said that the gem was worth nothing. If he refused to pay, Kroh Dee might ruin his reputation. On the other hand, if he gave it back to Kroh Dee, he would have to forfeit five 'chang' to the Lao, and that was out of the question. A moment's thought told him that there was only one way out of the difficulty. So, turning to Kroh Dee, he said: "Oh, you're asking about that stone of yours. Well, I have been examining it again, and I have now changed my mind. It's quite a good one, and, if you like, I will buy it from you."

"But you said before that it was only worth a 'fuang'," exclaimed Kroh Dee.

"Yes, I know I did, but I have changed my mind."

"Well, how much will you give me for it?" said Kroh Dee.

"Oh, I'll give you the price you were asking."

"All right, but don't you go about saying afterwards that I swindled you into buying a worthless stone for ten 'chang'."

"No," said Phra Chamnān, "I'm quite satisfied about it now," and therewith he counted out ten 'chang' to Kroh Dee, who put the money in his pocket and departed.

Phra Chamnān thought, of course, that he was making an excellent bargain, and waited impatiently for the seven days to expire. But the seven days went by, and eight, and nine, and ten, and still no Lao appeared. Then his heart began to sink within him, for, though he had the five 'chang' which the Lao had left as a guarantee and had now forfeited, his gorge rose at the thought of the ten 'chang' he had given to Kroh Dee for a worthless piece of glass. There was a clear loss of five 'chang'.

Still the days went by without any sign of the Lao, and at last Phra Chamnān realized that he had been the victim of a clever trick at the hands of Kroh Dee, and that he, the gem-dealer with the highest reputation in Bangkok, had been made to pay ten 'chang' to an ignorant rascal for a bottle-stopper which he had himself stated to be worth a 'fuang'. And yet no action could he take without exposing himself to the ridicule of the whole town.

So there he sits in gloomy silence, still waiting for the Lao to return.

NOTE BY PHYA MANUNET BANHĀN.—This story is a good example to show us how Greed, once it has entered our hearts, can cause us the heaviest losses; and how it can reduce us to such a state of foolishness, that all the wisdom we have laboriously acquired goes entirely by the board.

Look at our noble dealer in gems, the cleverest in the city. Who would credit him with being such a fool as to pay ten 'chang' for a worthless bottle-stopper!

VI

THE SKULLS' INTRIGUE

ABOUT the year 1450 of the Christian era, or a hundred years after Ayudhya had become the Capital City of Siam, there were three young men of good family living in the town of Kampengpet who, being solemnly linked together in the bond of friendship, came down to the Capital and presented themselves at the Palace for admission into the King's service. Of these three young men, one announced that he was skilled in the art of eating, the second in that of sleeping, and the third in the gentle art of love-making.

The King ordered each to be put to the proof of his skill, and those who had boasted of their prowess in the arts of eating and sleeping passed the tests provided without difficulty, but it was not so easy to find a suitable test for Nai Chao Choo, the young man who wished to be known as a successful love-maker. At length the King discovered that living in Ayudhya was a young lady, the widow of a prosperous citizen, who had the reputation of being very careful of her name and honour. Her late husband had always gone in fear of her virtue, and had submitted himself to her will. Never had he thought of taking any lesser wives, and in the end he had his reward, for his wife came to love him deeply, and even after his death still firmly believed that his astral body haunted the house. So much so that, although he had been dead for three years, and although she was still young and passing fair, she refused to consider the idea of marrying again, and went about her house as if her husband were still alive and communing with her. So jealously did she guard her name and reputation that she would never allow any man of her own station in life to cross her threshold, and this in spite of the fact that many a King's officer and many a wealthy man presented himself for her hand. They were one and all chased from her door with scant ceremony.

Having made this discovery, the King sent for Chao Choo and commanded him to lay siege to this lady's heart, and endeavour to win her for his wife. Chao Choo received the Royal Command with due obeisance and undertook to submit himself to the test.

His first step was to make, by instituting secret inquiries, a discreet and careful reconnaissance as to the lady's conduct and habits of life, not only while her late lamented husband was still alive, but also since she had been left his inconsolable widow. When he had satisfied himself that he was fully equipped with the knowledge necessary for his task, his next step was to obtain the skull of a woman which he placed in a small lacquered basket, together with an old 'panung' and 'pahom', the customary clothes which a wife would wear. Then, having been granted by the King the sum of eighty ticals and an old dilapidated sampan with a single paddle, he set out to procure all the goods and provisions he required for the purpose which he had in view: cooking-pots for his curry and rice, a charcoal stove, a frying-pan, with husked rice, fresh and salted fish, vegetables and betel-nut. These he placed in a second large basket, and having put both the baskets into his sampan, he started off down the river for the house of adventure. He himself was dressed in much-worn, tattered clothes, with an old palm-hat on his head. By chance, when he reached the lady's house, which bordered the river's bank and was built in the ancient style with a small roofed verandah overhanging the water, a heavy shower of rain began to fall, and Chao Choo took shelter in his boat beneath the verandah. At this moment the lady happened to come out of the house on to the verandah, and observing Chao Choo, asked him what he was doing there. Chao Choo thereupon held up his hands in dutiful greeting, and asked permission to take shelter until the storm had ceased. Seeing that he appeared to be merely a humble pedlar with no possible pretensions to becoming a suitor for her hand, the lady took pity upon Chao Choo, and graciously allowed him to rest beneath the verandah. As dusk drew on and the rain continued, Chao Choo began to make preparations in his boat for his evening meal, but all the time he was keeping a careful eye on the house above him through a wide crack in the floor. Presently the lady, who had withdrawn, came back on to the verandah to enjoy the cool air, and was immediately aware of Chao Choo cooking his rice and curry. Looking through the hole in the floor, to her astonishment she saw that he was preparing food for two persons and laying out two bowls for his rice. At the same time she heard him muttering and whispering to himself. Straining her ears, she caught a few words which came floating up, and distinctly heard him say: "My dear one, you are always with me. In the old days we used to take our food together, and now, whenever I sit down to eat, I never cease to think of you." As he spoke to himself, he took the rice out of the pot, and put a portion into each of the two bowls he had set before him.

The lady was mystified beyond measure, and, knowing that Chao Choo had come in his boat alone, wondered whom on earth he could be addressing. Looking more closely, she suddenly saw Chao Choo lift a skull out of the basket beside him and set it gently down by the bowl which he had placed immediately opposite to his own, and, as he did so, speak to it in endearing terms: "Come, dear heart, come and take your food with me, and let us be together even as in the old days when you were still alive." When she saw Chao Choo communing with the skull in front of him, the lady's quick mind at once grasped the fact that it must be his dead wife to whom he was speaking, and at her own sad thoughts her throat was caught with sobs. She thought to herself: "How he must have loved her. That is what I call a true husband, one after my own heart. For, wherever he goes, he takes the skull of his wife with him, just as I keep my husband's skull in my own house, to live and eat with me."

Now all the time that Chao Choo was going through this performance he was peeping at the lady out of the corner of his eye, for he knew that she was watching him. When he had finished his meal, he gathered up the skull and the clothes with it and put them away in the basket again, so that the skull could not be seen. Then he placed the basket by his side and lay down and groaned, sticking some betel-leaves on his temples as if he had a violent headache.

Thus for some time he lay, but at night-fall he rose up and called out to the lady of the house that he was not feeling very well, and asked her permission to stay under the verandah for that night, to which the lady in her compassion readily agreed.

When morning came, Chao Choo arose very shakily, with dull movements, as if he were still feeling unwell. Overcome by her curiosity, the lady stole out again in her bare feet to watch him through the hole in the verandah floor, and, knowing that she was there, Chao Choo brought out the skull from the basket and went through exactly the same performance as on the previous evening. As she watched, her compassion increased all the more, and thinking that he was really indisposed, she allowed Chao Choo to remain until he should be fully recovered. Every time he took his meals, she came out to watch and spy upon him, until at length, when two full days had gone by, she put her head over the balcony of the verandah and said to Chao Choo: "If you are still feeling ill and not able to travel, please come up and rest in a little room I can give you close to the verandah. You will be much more comfortable there than in your boat."

With many protestations of thanks, Chao Choo accepted the offer gratefully, and carried all his belongings with the basket containing the skull up into the room near the verandah. Once installed, Chao Choo made great play in pretending to hide the basket containing the skull, and behaved himself with such gentleness, and acted the part of a sick man so well, that the lady was completely deceived, and thought he must be genuinely ill.

Indeed, the mere fact that he was carrying the skull of his dead wife about with him, which, as the lady said to herself, no other man in the world but her own husband would have done, made a great impression upon her stony but feminine heart, and she became very concerned about Chao Choo's condition. Softly she asked him: "What is actually the matter with you?" to which Chao Choo as softly replied: "Oh, it is an old ailment of mine. It always lasts for some time, but eventually I shall recover." On hearing this, the lady offered Chao Choo all kinds of medicine to drink, which he accepted with a seemingly grateful heart. In the meantime he still continued to bring out the skull secretly to share his meals with him, knowing well that the lady was as secretly watching him, and addressed it with such endearing words as he knew would appeal to the lady's heart.

In the course of a few days he arranged his affairs so well and so cunningly, and behaved with such uncommon respect and good sense, that he began to excite not only curiosity and compassion, but a more lively regard in the lady's bosom, almost, as it might be said, against her will and desire; proving clearly what the ancients say, that the more you pretend to hide something from the eyes of others, the more you excite their curiosity to see it. The consequence was that he received many attentions and comforts from the lady herself in the shape of medicine, food, and clothes, and all the servants, who were of course female, used to come and converse with him, whenever they found the opportunity. In this way Chao Choo was soon on the friendliest terms with all the inmates of the house, and in the course of time he became on particularly good terms with one of the girls who was her mistress's favourite servant and enjoyed all her confidences. One day, when he saw a favourable chance, he opened his heart to this girl and promised to reward her with the sum of eighty ticals if she would only purloin the skull which her mistress kept so carefully and secretly in her bedroom and hand it over to him. He guaranteed that, whatever the outcome of the affair, he would shield her from all punishment. On this condition the girl promised to obey his wishes, and that same night, while her mistress was asleep, she carried off the skull of the lady's husband from her bedroom and gave it into Chao Choo's keeping. As soon as he received it, Chao Choo put it carefully away in the same basket with the other skull and went to sleep again.

The next morning he rose up early and began to prepare his curry and rice, and, when his meal was ready, he set out two bowls for his wife and himself as usual, at the same time summoning her in a voice sufficiently loud to be heard by the eavesdropper outside: "Come, my dear, your food is ready, come and take your meal with me, just as you used to do when you were alive." With this he stretched out his hand to lift out the skull, but as he was feeling about in the basket he suddenly cried out: "What is this!" Rising up with a gesture expressive of great surprise, he bent over the basket and examined it carefully, and then angrily exclaimed: "So this is what you have been doing, is it? I thought I heard a noise in the night; it must have been you rolling about. This is too much. It's scandalous, and I will not endure it."

Hearing Chao Choo talking in this strange, excitable fashion, the lady of the house crept closer to the partition of the room where Chao Choo was and looked through a chink in the wall. As she did so she heard Chao Choo say: "It's four years now since you died, and all that time I have been faithful to you and never thought of taking another wife. Whatever difficulties I have had to encounter, I have never failed to carry you about with me, and we have eaten and lived and slept together just the same as when you were still alive. Indeed, I have never considered myself a widower, and now what have you done? Here we have been only seven days in this house, and you must go and seduce the skull of this good lady's husband. Is that a small thing to do? How can I forgive you? This is clearly the end of our common merit together. From this hour we must each pursue our own 'karma' alone. Take your lover and go, you are henceforth no wife of mine."

As he spoke he lifted both the skulls out of the basket and placed them on the ground. Glaring at them with a terrible mien, he held a bowl of water before him, and as he poured the water drop by drop, he called upon the gods and angels to witness that his wife had been faithless to him, and prayed that, in whatever future state he might find himself, he might be granted a wife as faithful to him as he had been to his, and that he might never again encounter such a treacherous mate as his late one had been. His prayer completed, he searched about in the basket holding his cooking-pots for a knife, delaying his search long enough for the lady to recognize clearly the skull of her husband, and then, finding the knife he sought, he lifted it above his head and smashed both the skulls in pieces. Having finished his gruesome task to his satisfaction, he gathered up the pieces in one of the baskets and flung the whole into the river.

Now, as related above, the lady of the house was watching closely all that Chao Choo was doing. She saw him take both the skulls out of the basket, and, recognizing that one of them was her late husband, at once firmly believed that the latter's spirit had deceived her and had been making love to the spirit of Chao Choo's dead wife. Woman-like, she went hot all over with rage at the thought that she had been betrayed by one whom she had loved so jealously and long, and her eyes were filled with angry tears. All her love for her late husband vanished, and at the bottom of her heart she felt happy and glad that Chao Choo had smashed his skull and pitched it into the river. Such was her faith that she believed that her husband and Chao Choo's wife would one day be born again and come together as husband and wife, thus making an end of her own love for her husband, and leaving her free to marry again if she so should wish.

Going stealthily back to her own bedroom, she tore down all the hangings, the pillows, the little shrine—

everything in fact that she had kept sacred to the memory of her late husband, and cast them all away. And as she lay down on her own bed, she could not dismiss the thoughts that kept crowding into her active, busy mind, thoughts that constantly brought before her a comparison of her late husband and the poor fellow who was sleeping in the room near by, much to the former's disparagement.

It was clear to her that, although she had preserved her love for her husband's spirit with as great care and devotion as when he himself was alive, the latter had taken the first opportunity offered him to leave her and make love to the spirit of another man's wife, not like the poor man who had come to stay with her and who had kept his faith towards his wife intact, even though the latter had been dead for four years. As for that husband of hers—there was not the slightest doubt that, if she had died before him, the wretch would have had a score of new wives by this time; but that dear fellow next door, there was no thought in *his* mind of taking another wife.

And this was naturally followed by another thought. Now that Chao Choo had parted company with his wife's spirit, and she with her husband's, where could she find a truer and more faithful spouse than this one who had proved his worth so clearly, that is, of course, if she really wanted to marry again. If he could be so faithful to his late wife's memory, would he not be even more faithful to her, who was equally true to her late husband, and who was still young and beautiful? As for his poverty and his condition, was that not an advantage in disguise? Was it not a fact that most wealthy men always took a number of lesser wives in addition to their principal one, and that it did not bring the latter any greater happiness on earth? It was the nature of human beings to try and seek happiness in this life. Some people thought that happiness depended entirely on wealth; others saw happiness in independence of mind and body. But she herself had abundance of property and wealth. She had no desire or need of a wealthy husband. What she wanted more than anything else was a man of the same disposition and feelings as herself, one who would be faithful and incline to her wishes, and such a man was far harder to find than one with mere riches.

Thus she lay with her thoughts till dawn, when she made up her mind that she must have the man next door to be her husband, and, the circumstances being propitious, the matter was as easy to arrange as paddling a canoe downstream. It did not take very long before Chao Choo realized the emotions he had roused in the lady's breast, and their friendship gradually and daily grew to intimacy, just as the magnet attracts the steel. As soon as he thought the time was ripe, Chao Choo declared his love, and the lady responding without demur, the two became husband and wife.

Thus Chao Choo achieved his aim and carried out the King's command, but whether the couple found happiness or sorrow in their conjugal life together is beyond the province of this tale, and must be left to the reader's imagination. We can only offer them our hopes and prayers.

vii

THE LOVE LESSON

"As swift as a crow, as bold as a woman."—Old Siamese Proverb

NOT far from the town of Petchaburi there once lived a young man named Nai Samret, who had reached the age when curiosity began to stir in him a desire to study and learn the wiles and devices of womankind. So, taking a notebook in his hand, he set out, after the manner of his countrymen, to find a counsellor and guide who might expound to him the many traps and pitfalls which the fair sex lays for unwary man.

One afternoon, while on his quest, Nai Samret was passing by a certain garden, when he happened to espy the wife of the owner, a comely young woman of twenty-five, pulling up vegetables in a plot of ground which stood at some distance from the house.

Nang Lamert, for such was the lady's name, was quick to notice Nai Samret coming along the path outside the garden fence, and called out to him in a casual but friendly manner: "Where are you going, young man, and what are you looking for?"

Nai Samret looked up, and, seeing an attractive girl in the garden, called back: "If you wish to know, I have a keen desire to learn the wiles of women, and I am searching for a 'Kru' who can teach me their artful ways."

Now Nai Samret, who was a fine, upstanding young man, found favour in Nang Lamert's eyes, and she saucily replied:

"If that's the case, you have no need to go any farther. I know a good deal more about my own sex than any of your old 'Kru.' Why not take a few lessons from me?"

As he gazed at her face and form, Nai Samret agreed with a cheerful heart and begged to become her pupil.

"Then," said Nang Lamert, "why not begin now? Come inside and let us find a shady corner of the garden, where no one will disturb us at our lessons."

Nothing loth, Nai Samret entered the garden, and together they found a hidden nook, safe from prying eyes. And such was the mutual attraction between the two of them that in one lesson he learnt more of the ways of women than all the 'Kru' in the world could have taught him in a score of years.

In her eagerness to teach and his to learn the hours slipped all too quickly by, and suddenly Nang Lamert cried: "Good gracious, the sun is going down; I must fly, or my husband will miss me. But if you like, little man, I will show you presently a trick worth knowing. Do you know what I will do? I will introduce you to my husband, and to-night we will occupy the same room together, with my husband in the room next to us, and without his knowing who we are. So stay here until I come and fetch you."

With this Nang Lamert jumped up and ran back to the house. Finding her husband at home, she went up to him with a smile on her face, and when he asked her what the joke was, said: "Oh, it's nothing much—only when I was pulling up some vegetables in the garden just now, I gave one of the roots too sudden a jerk and overbalanced and fell on my back. Just look at me, I'm covered with dirt. Do be a dear and dust me down."

The husband, poor simple soul, burst out laughing, and getting a cloth carefully dusted his wife's back, for which she thanked him prettily and went off to her housework.

A little later on Nang Lamert sought out her husband

again, and, appearing to recollect something she had forgotten, said:

"Oh, by the way, I quite forgot to tell you, while I was in the garden this afternoon, Nang Chuang, my niece, called to tell me that my mother was not very well and wanted me to go and see her. If you don't mind, I think I'll go along now; but if it's nothing really serious, I'll come back this evening as early as I can. Mind you look after the baby while I'm away."

Her husband raised no objection, only telling her not to be too late; so Nang Lamert handed over the baby to his care and went off to find Nai Samret, who was still hiding all this time in the shady corner.

She explained to him exactly what she was going to do and the part he had to play, and then, when an hour or two had passed in converse on the pleasant theme of love, and it had grown quite dark, they went back to the house together. Just before they arrived Nang Lamert took a 'pahom' and covered up her head and face so that no one could see who she was, and made Nai Samret walk in front. At the foot of the steps leading up to the house Nai Samret called out to the husband who was inside, and when the latter came out to see who was there, asked him: "Is Nang Lamert at home?"

The husband replied shortly: "No, she is out," and was about to retire, but before he could do so Nai Samret continued quickly: "I am a cousin of Nang Lamert's, you know; her mother, Nang Cheua, is my aunt. This morning Nang Chuang came and told us that Nang Cheua was ill, and asked us to go and see her. We were on our way to visit her now, but I thought I would give Nang Lamert the news as I passed, and ask her to come with us, if she liked, so that we could all go together."

Hearing Nai Samret speak so trippingly of Nang Lamert and her relations, and refer to Nang Chuang, who he supposed had just visited his wife as well, the husband believed that Nai Samret actually was a cousin of Nang Lamert's, and, inviting him to enter the house, ran off to fetch a lamp to light the way. But when he came back, Nai Samret, who had entered the house with Nang Lamert, said: "Oh, please don't light a lamp. My wife, who is with me here, has inflammation of the eyes, and is almost blind. She has only come with me because she believes that Aunt Cheua is seriously ill. She cannot bear a light, it hurts her eyes so much."

The husband did not doubt him for a moment, so he put out the lamp, and for some little time they sat and talked in the dark. Nang Lamert took good care to hide herself as much as possible behind Nai Samret, and sat on the floor with her head bent and well covered up; and as her husband had no suspicion of her in his mind, he did not look at her at all carefully to see what she was like.

When he learnt from the husband that Nang Lamert had already gone to visit her mother, Nai Samret became rather uncertain as to what they should do, and eventually the husband invited them both to stay the night and go on their visit in the morning. "After all," he said, "Nang Lamert is with her mother, and it's rather late for you to go now." After some hesitation and reluctance, Nai Samret and his 'wife' agreed to stay, and the husband arranged the outer room for them to sleep in, while he himself occupied the inner room with the baby. And presently they all went quietly to bed, and Nang Lamert gave another lesson in woman's wiles to her not unwilling pupil. But in the middle of the night the baby awoke and began to cry. This woke up its mother in the next room at once, and in her anxiety she aroused the young man sleeping by her. After a few minutes whispering together Nai Samret called out to the husband in the inner room: "My wife has an infant child as well just now, and if you would care for her to do so, she says that she will gladly come in and nurse the baby." The husband expressed his pleasure at hearing this, and so Nang Lamert rose up and went into her husband's room and soon comforted the baby and put it to sleep again. She spoke no word, but as she was leaving the room she purposely passed close by her husband and brushed against him. This was too much for the husband, who grasped her by the wrist and tried to pull her towards him. But Nang Lamert at once gave him a push, and, wrenching herself free, ran back into the outer room. There she sank down by Nai Samret's side and began to whisper to him in such an audible tone that her husband could not help hearing all that she said. Realizing to the full what he had done, the wretched fellow spent the rest of the night wide awake, torn between desire and shame.

Towards the dawn Nang Lamert and Nai Samret rose and called out to the husband that they ought to be going and begged him to excuse them. This came as a great relief to the husband, as he had no desire to wait until daylight and meet them face to face after the little affair of the previous night; so he called out good-bye from the inside room and excused himself for not coming out to see them off for fear of waking the baby.

The pair of them then left the house, and when they reached the garden, Nang Lamert shyly went up to Nai Samret, and looking up at him, said: "Well now, is that not a good trick that I showed you last night, and have I not taught you a great deal about women in a very short time? Perhaps, if you are a good boy, I will give you another lesson a little later on. But you must go now, or we shall be caught. Good-bye till the next time."

With that she dismissed Nai Samret, but she herself waited in the garden until daylight, and then went back to her husband. At the sight of his anxious, shameful face she could scarcely restrain herself from laughing, but, true to her part, she sprang at him, pretending to be furious with rage, and reviled him, saying: "You wretch! I've heard all about you. Don't you believe you can cover it up. Just because I happen to be away for a night, and my young cousin and his wife come and stay here, you must needs go and try to assault her. Oh, you beast! and especially when she was helping to nurse our baby, thinking no possible harm could come to her as one of the family. You're not fit to live with; but you men are all the same where a woman is concerned. I hate you!"

The poor husband did not know what to say or do. He could not deny the accusation, because he knew it to be true, and he felt sure that Nai Samret and his wife had told Nang Lamert all about it. So he could only look very sheepish and, with much contrition, beg his wife to forgive him. Which, after a certain interval and with much condescension, she graciously consented to do.

NOTE BY PHYA MANUNET BANHĀN.—This story is a good example of the maxim which runs that, when once a wife has taken a lover, she will attack her husband with a shameless, brazen heart. As the old saying goes, "As swift as a crow and as bold as a woman."

viii

CELESTIALS IN CONTRAST

ABOUT fifty years ago there were in Swatow two poor Chinamen named Nguan Heng and Hah Yong, who lived in the same street and were close, intimate friends. Finding only a scanty means of livelihood in their own native land, they agreed to go and seek their fortune in Siam. They managed to scrape together enough money to pay the fares demanded by a coasting junk, but otherwise they quitted their country penniless, with no other worldly possessions than the clothes they wore.

Leaving their own inhospitable land behind them, for the first time in their lives they crossed the mighty ocean and came to the shores of the Gulf of Siam. As the junk sailed lazily along the coast, they saw in the distance the wealth of bright green rice-fields and all around the spreading trees welcoming them with outstretched arms, and they conjured up in their minds a vision of abundance and prosperity such as they had never heard or dreamt of before. Never had they seen cultivable land so suited to their nimble minds and hands, and their faces shone with pleasure at the thought that they had decided to come and seek their fortune in this happy, smiling land.

As they wound their way up the River Menam and approached the port of Bangkok, they agreed to separate, each to seek the fortune that fate should bring him; but before they parted they made to each other a solemn promise that, until he had amassed a sum of not less than fifty 'chang,' neither of them would eat pork, or duck, or fowl. Then the ship having come to anchor, they said good-bye and went their several ways.

Now Nguan Heng was true to his word. From the moment he landed he applied himself diligently to honest, manly toil. He refrained from indulging in any kind of luxury, and took for his sustenance nothing but rice and salt and pickled turnip. Whatever money he earned he put laboriously by and spent as little as he humanly could. And so the time went by. In a few years, owing to his thrifty habits and to the restraint he exercised in food and drink, he found himself the proud possessor of a small capital, with which he began to trade. Still his thrifty habits persisted, and his little capital grew and grew, until it was not a great many years before Nguan Heng became one of the prosperous merchants of the kingdom. Land he had, and a house, and with his wife and children led a happy, busy, contented life. But it was not until he had a hundred 'chang' put safely by that his mind turned to any thought of luxury. It was only when he found that his daily income was more than enough to supply himself and his family, not only with the necessities of life but with some of its luxuries as well, that he consented to spend his money on pork, or ducks, or fowls.

Now we must turn to Hah Yong, the friend of his youth, and see what became of him.

When Hah Yong parted from Nguan Heng, the promise he had given was strong in his mind, and for some time he pursued an industrious, thrifty life. He kept ever before him the well-tried maxim that luxury and sloth are bosom friends, and whatever he earned was put scrupulously by.

But by and by there came an evil day. One afternoon as he was walking in the market, he happened to see a duck exposed for sale that had died of some disease, and for this reason was being marketed at a cheaper price than the salt fish he was accustomed to buy. At once the thought sprang to his mind: "Of course we made that promise together not to eat pork, or ducks, or fowls, because we knew that they were luxuries and could only be bought at a dearer price than fish. But here we have the reverse. The promise cannot apply in this case, and, if I buy this duck, it cannot be held a breach of our agreement." Besides, he had not eaten duck for many moons. So he bought the duck and ate it, and the taste of it, after his long abstinence, was so delicious, that the next day the craving for more took hold of him, and he went out into the market again to see if he could find another duck that was sold at a cheaper price than fish. By a lucky chance he found one and promptly bought it. But this time, as he ate the duck, the flesh was not quite so toothsome as on the first day, and he said to himself: "There's no doubt about it, a duck that has died of disease is not such good eating as one that has been killed." At once the desire came into his heart to taste a duck that had been killed, and the next day, his craving growing stronger and stronger, he could not resist the temptation to go into the market and buy one, "only to compare the taste", as he said. But the taste was so immeasurably more delicious, that it soon became a regular dish in Hah Yong's daily fare, until at length he tired of duck, and his stomach turned to thoughts of other kinds of dishes. Chickens were there, pork was there. Chickens were good, pork was good, and it was not long before Hah Yong had broken the terms of his promise in letter and in spirit to his stomach's content. And so it came about that Hah Yong's daily food began to cost more than what he earned, not to mention the cost of lodging and clothes and all the other expenses which life entailed for him; and soon he found it necessary to draw upon the store of money that he had so carefully saved in his earlier days. At length that store was gone and only the craving for luxuries remained.

As he could now no longer satisfy this craving, his mind turned to his friend, Nguan Heng, and he determined to go and seek him out, for he knew, from reports he had heard, that the latter by this time had prospered exceedingly, and he thought that perhaps Nguan Heng might allow him to live with him. Without delay he set out for Nguan Heng's house, and there he made a full confession of how he had broken the promise and placed himself at his friend's mercy.

Nguan Heng received Hah Yong kindly, for he had not forgotten their early friendship. He gave him a small hut in his compound to live in, and twice a day, morning and evening, he sent him rice and salt fish for his food.

Now in Nguan Heng's garden there was a large number of tamarind trees, whose leaves, when boiled, make succulent eating. A thought flashed through Nguan Heng's mind, and one day he sent for Hah Yong and told him that he might choose the smallest tamarind tree in the garden, and pick the leaves to boil with his rice and fish. With a grateful heart Hah Yong selected a tree, and every day plucked the leaves from the branches and ate them with his scanty meals. In time the tree naturally became bare, and Hah Yong, having no more tamarind leaves to eat, went off to his friend to ask permission to select another tree. Nguan Heng gave his ready consent, but this time told Hah Yong to pick out the largest tree he could find.

When Hah Yong had been picking the leaves from the largest tree for about the same length of time as he had done from the smallest tree, Nguan Heng sent for him and asked him how he was getting on, and whether he now found his supply of leaves sufficient for his needs. To which Hah Yong replied that now he had enough and more than enough. He could turn from one branch to another, and by the time he had finished a quarter of the tree, the branches he had stripped were coming into leaf again.

Then his friend, Nguan Heng, spoke to him seriously and said: "Now just consider these two tamarind trees, and think of what you have been doing. Before the small one had time to establish itself firmly and grow up into a large abundant tree, you had eaten all its leaves and exhausted its resources. In a short time it was bare, exactly like yourself. Just at the time when you ought to have been husbanding all your strength and money, you were spending more than you earned on nothing but food and luxuries. It did not take very long before you found yourself at the end of your tether, with poverty staring you in the face. Now turn to the largest tree, which was fully grown, and whose branches were developed with abundance of leaves. You could pick and eat them every day, and still fresh ones were always bursting forth before you could exhaust its supplies. Is not that like myself, who have built up a business, and by thrift and self-denial now have more than enough to buy whatever luxuries of food I desire, without having to eat into my capital to do so. Take this as a lesson, and see if you cannot retrieve your hopes of fortune."

Note by Phya Manunet Banhān.—This story is meant as a warning to us all. If we give ourselves up to luxury and indulge in delicate foods, the craving for them will only go on increasing without end; and if our expenditure is more than, or even equal to, our income, in the end we shall find ourselves faced with poverty. At that time, if some illness or disaster should overtake us, then much suffering will be our inevitable lot. And if we are reduced to suffering and hardships through poverty, it may easily lead us into a life of crime.

ix

THE KEEPER OF THE BOOK

I HAVE heard the story told that, if we reckon eighty-five years back from the year R.S. 131,[1] there lived in Bangkok a Head Priest, who belonged to the Thammayut sect of the Brotherhood. He was looked upon with the greatest respect, as one who had a profound belief in the Three Gems, and it might indeed be said of him that he was a true follower of the Lord Buddha.

One day the Head Priest was recounting his experiences to another Head Priest, and this is the story he related.

"As I lay asleep one night, just before dawn, I had a singular dream. In my dream I saw four beings of gigantic form, with curly hair, and wearing the silk 'panung' with sashes of the jack-fruit pattern as in the days of old, enter my cell, bearing between them on their shoulders a Book far larger than the Book of Pra Malai, and with its cover beautifully bound in gold. As they approached my mat, I half rose up and asked them for what purpose they came to seek me. The four men set down the Book and answered all together: 'We have come to hand over this Book to you to be its Keeper for the future.' On my demanding to know the nature of the Book, they all replied again as one: 'Every human soul who dies of cholera has his name entered in this Book.' Then I asked them: 'Do you wish me to take over my duties and receive this Book while I am still a living being, or after I am dead?' They all answered with one voice: 'You must die of cholera, and then you shall be

[1] The year R.S. 131 is equivalent to A.D. 1912–13, being reckoned from the founding of Bangkok in 1782. This era is no longer in use.

the Keeper of the Book.' Then I said to them: 'But to die of cholera is a very painful death, may I not die from some other cause?' The reply came stern and swift: 'You *must* die of cholera, only thus can you become the Keeper of the Book.' Then I thought to myself: 'It is clear that death is at hand and that I need have no further hold on life. But if I die now and receive the Book I will burn it to ashes. By so doing, no further human soul will die of cholera, and I shall have conferred some benefit upon my fellow-men.'

"With this thought in my mind, I turned to the four gigantic men and said: 'Very well, I am willing to die of cholera, as you require; so you may hand the Book over into my keeping.' But the four men had read my thoughts as if I had spoken them, and answered: 'This is a very ancient Book, and you shall not burn it, as you think to do. You cannot deceive us so, and you are not worthy to be its Keeper. We must go and seek the second priest in charge of this Monastery.' With these words they lifted the great Book on to their shoulders and went out, leaving me alone in my cell.

"So frightened was I at the dream that I woke with a start just as dawn appeared, and such was the force of suggestion that I at once became seriously ill. So ill, indeed, that I felt sure I was suffering from cholera. Yet presently the pains ceased and in a few hours I recovered. But when I was well enough to go and visit the second priest, I found him lying dead in his cell. He had died of cholera soon after dawn."

Note by Phya Manunet Banhān.—We may well believe that the dream which the Head Priest experienced might easily become a reality, for we have his own evidence that the second priest died of cholera, even as the dream foretold, and that he himself became seriously ill. Thus it serves to show us that, although the demerit which the Head Priest had made in his past lives might have blotted out all the credit which he had gained in this life, that is, as a human being, yet the merit which he acquired by showing mercy and charity towards the whole of mankind (namely, by his secret thought to burn the Book) had greater power than his previous demerit. In this way the Head Priest was enabled to live to a ripe old age and to uphold the Church and the Three Gems for many fruitful years.

It is clear then that we all possess a 'Karma' which we build up both in our past lives and in our present. It is ours and ours alone, and follows us like the shadow the body. According as either side is greater than the other, so we reap in proportion to the force of the 'Karma', whether good or bad, which we have built up.

X

THE BURIED FIGURES, OR THE POWER OF SUGGESTION

"*Listen, Reflect, Ask, Write.*"—OLD SIAMESE PROVERB

ONCE upon a time in the town of Chieng Rai there lived a young girl of remarkable beauty, named Meh Chan. As she ripened to womanhood, no other maiden could equal, or even compare, with her for grace of form or perfection of feature. Her slender, lissome figure, and her gently rounded bosom, so well set off by her silken 'sin' [1] and tight-fitting jacket, and crowned by her large, laughing eyes, were a joy to behold. Withal, she was as virtuous as she was beautiful, and 'earthward bent her modest look'; and as her parents, though of humble origin, had achieved a position of independence, she soon became a theme for song and praise in all the country round.

By the time she had reached the age of eighteen, all the young men, of every rank and station in life, had fallen in love with her, and were tumbling over one another in their endeavour to gain possession of the coveted prize. The old 'go-betweens' had never been kept so busy in all their lives. And yet, in spite of their striving, she favoured none of the young men, and her heart remained free as the birds that fly.

Now at this time in a temple near by there dwelt a young man named Ai Foo, who was the personal attendant of the Head Priest, a man of learning and great renown as a distiller of love potions and powerful charms. Indeed, such was the respect and repute in which the Head Priest was held by all the people of the town, that it was firmly believed that, even though a couple had

[1] Skirt.

separated in anger for as long as three years or more, he possessed the power of reconciling their differences and of bringing them together in love and amity once again.

Presently Ai Foo, who regarded the Head Priest as his father, fell in love with Meh Chan, and having found an old woman to act as his go-between, sent her to find out if there was any possible chance for his suit. But Meh Chan would have none of him. She had numbers of wooers far more agreeable and suitable in every way, although she still could say that no one as yet had found his way to her heart.

Yet the old 'go-between', like many another, was growing tired of this unprofitable game, and returned and told Ai Foo that Meh Chan was secretly in love with him. All unsuspecting, Ai Foo believed her, and became so puffed up with pride that he could not keep the secret, but went about among his friends boasting that he, of all the young men of the town, was the acknowledged lover of Meh Chan.

It was not long before friends brought this news to Meh Chan and her father and mother. Meh Chan was furious with rage, as only a girl can be, and reviled Ai Foo as a worthless rascal, spreading untruths and boastful stories about her, saying to her mother, "as if I would so much as look at a boy like Ai Foo." Then shame and the ribald laughter of his own friends took hold of Ai Foo, and he burnt so hot within him, that he in his turn became inflamed with anger against Meh Chan, to a degree that he scarcely dared to walk past her house for fear he should catch sight of her and do her some injury.

This little affair had one important effect, however. It made Meh Chan realize that, if she wished to avoid any further trouble, she had better choose a husband quickly out of the many suitors around her. So at last she made her choice, and, after the customary visits had been exchanged between her own and the bridegroom's family, her father and mother fixed the day for her marriage and sent invitations to their relatives and friends to attend it.

When this came to the ears of Ai Foo, as it very soon did, his heart became more inflamed with anger than ever, and he determined, if he could, to prevent the marriage. So he sent word by a friend of the family that, if they persisted in marrying her to the chosen bridegroom, he would get his Head Priest to give her a love philtre, and at the same time to make little waxen figures of himself and Meh Chan embracing one another, bind them together, and bury them in the ground with all the necessary incantations. This would soon make her change her mind and bring her back to him. If she would consent to have him as her husband, he would ask the Head Priest, as soon as they were married, to remove the spell. But if she still refused to marry him, he would get the Priest to do it again and again, until in the end she would go raving mad and finally die.

The threat lost nothing in the telling. With much relish and detail the friend of the family pictured to the trembling girl, in her parents' presence, the diabolical skill which the Head Priest possessed, and the success which always attended his efforts, as they themselves knew only too well from the experience of others.

There was no doubt about the effect. From the moment they heard Ai Foo's threat, their faces changed and their spirits fell. A deep anxiety entered the parents' minds, and a feeling pervaded the house that something evil was about to happen. They watched their daughter's face and form, and dreaded to find some subtle change coming over her. To their credit, neither they nor Meh Chan would hear or think of obeying Ai Foo, but they had to keep on the safe side, and they hastily postponed the marriage fixed, holding out no hope to the bridegroom as to when, if ever, the wedding could take place.

In the course of a month or two, however, finding that nothing had happened, the parents' fears began to abate and their natural spirits to return. Not so Meh Chan's. On the contrary, as the days went by, her fears gained ever more ground. She was really a very gentle girl, with the soft heart of a true maiden; besides, she was very, very young, and she firmly believed that Ai Foo could and would carry out his threat, with all its dire results. So as her anxiety grew greater, she became pallid and wan, her joyful laugh left her, and her eyes were often wet with tears. Eating, she thought of Ai Foo and his threat; sleeping, she dreamt of him. So constantly was the demon at her elbow that she never had time to forget him. She might be sitting down to a meal of some special delicacy her mother had set for her. Suddenly, in the act of lifting a morsel to her mouth, the picture of herself and Ai Foo would pass before her eyes; she would stop abruptly and put it down again. Her hunger left her, and no more food would pass her lips. Or perhaps she might be chatting almost gaily with her girl friends; suddenly they would see her face change from gay to grave. Her eyebrows would pucker and frown, and not another word would she utter. They knew that the shadow had come before her eyes.

In a short time Meh Chan was a changed girl, and her face the colour of a sheet. At times she would be fast asleep at night, and suddenly she would start up with a loud cry and implore her father and mother to come and help her; at others she would be sitting quietly sewing in the house, and suddenly for no reason burst into tears. In the course of time Meh Chan was so much changed from her normal healthy self that her father and mother became seriously alarmed, and called a meeting of all their relatives to see if something could be done to cheer her spirits, which had sunk so low.

They all agreed that she must be the victim of some powerful spell which had been cast upon her. Her body had become so thin, and her face, which once was beautiful like the full moon, had grown so dull and white and heavy—all these signs clearly showed the nature of her illness. If the spell was not removed quickly, she might even lose her reason.

Unfortunately for Meh Chan, the mere fact of her parents and relatives consulting together, and deciding that she was under a spell, only served to increase her self-inflicted punishment, and convinced her all the more that the symptoms that she felt in her heart were directly caused by a love philtre. So her pains and fears grew daily worse, until her strength was almost at an end, and she could neither eat nor sleep. Her condition at last became so bad that she lay like a log in her bedroom all day long without moving or speaking.

Her parents called in many doctors, who did what they could and gave her medicines to drink; but all to no purpose. When they heard the full story of her illness, they all agreed, too, that she was under the spell of a sorcerer, who had given her a love philtre and had buried her waxen image in the ground. So the astrologers were summoned, who sprinkled her with mystic words and holy water; but although her parents called in as many as could be found, all their charms and water proved in vain and no merit was found in them. Indeed, their only effect upon the girl was to implant her fears more firmly in her mind and to increase her terrors of the beyond. At last Meh Chan became so ill that her father and mother gave up all hopes of her recovery and prepared for the worst to happen.

Matters had reached this critical state, when it happened that an old and venerable wandering priest arrived in the town with his 'lūk sit',[1] and put up at a temple near the house of Meh Chan. Early in the morning following his arrival all the folk who lived near by, including the parents of Meh Chan, took their offerings of food to the old priest, and, as was their custom, asked his help in various ways—some for charms and amulets, others for holy water to sprinkle upon their houses. When it came to the turn of Meh Chan's parents, they poured out the tale of their daughter's woeful state, and begged him to give them some holy water to sprinkle on their child. The old priest listened intently and asked them many searching questions, until he knew the story from beginning to end. He at once guessed the truth, for he was a clear-thinking, wise old priest, well versed in the Buddhist Scriptures. He knew that the sole reason of the girl's illness was her mistaken belief that she was the victim of a spell. He knew, too, that all the charms and incantations which the astrologers were wont to use were of no value whatever and had no power to make people ill or well; but he said to himself, "It is no use my telling these foolish folk the truth, for their primitive beliefs are ingrained and fixed fast in their childish minds. Yet, if I say or do nothing, this poor girl will surely die; I must try and think out some plan by which to save her life."

He sat for some time in thoughtful silence, until at last an inspiration flashed through his mind, and he said to the parents: "In such a serious case as this, when the victim has been for so long under the spell, for me merely to give you holy water to sprinkle upon her is not enough to cure her. I must myself come within the limits of your house and offer up prayers with solemn rites. Only in this way can I save her."

[1] Disciple or 'chela'.

Seeing the good effect his simple words were already having, he continued: "You may not know it, but I have studied for many years all the various methods of breaking the spells of sorcerers, and may, without boasting, call myself an expert in the art. I have, in fact, already exorcised many such evil spirits. If I perform the prescribed rites and offer up the requisite prayers, I can call up the waxen figures that the sorcerer has buried, and they will come at my command."

The parents of Meh Chan and their friends, who were listening reverently to his words, bowed their heads to the ground in wonder and implored him to take her under his protection. The old priest willingly agreed to do so, but said: "First I must eat and free myself from all worldly thoughts and needs, and then I will come to your daughter's aid. In the meanwhile you must be preparing all things necessary for the ceremony I have to perform. Here is my begging-bowl. Fill it full of clear, pure water and set it in a place open to the skies. Next, take a white cloth of good quality, new and spotlessly clean, and place it over the mouth of the bowl. Then roll two candles and make them ready for me, each of the weight of one tical."

With this he dismissed the parents of Meh Chan, who returned to their house and busied themselves with the tasks allotted them. But the news spread like wildfire of what the old priest was about to do, and in a very short time all the neighbours and people round about, nearly a hundred in all, gathered together in front of Meh Chan's house, all agog with curiosity to see the priest summon up the waxen figures which lay buried in the earth, plain for them all to see.

As soon as the old priest was sure that he was alone, he summoned his 'lūk sit' and unfolded to him the trick he was about to play for Meh Chan's benefit, and rehearsed to him exactly the part that he, the 'lūk sit', had to perform.

For this purpose he took a small piece of hardened beeswax, heated it at a charcoal fire, and then cunningly fashioned the forms of a man and woman embracing one another. These forms, when bound together, although their outlines were clear, he made so small that his disciple could hide them under his longish finger-nail; and when they were finished to his liking, he gave them to the 'lūk sit' to keep.

As soon as the sun had passed the meridian, the old priest and his 'lūk sit' walked with sober gait to the house of Meh Chan, and came to rest in the grassless courtyard fronting it, where her parents were waiting to receive him. There he desired them to set a prayer-mat at the outer edge of the courtyard and, having taken his seat upon it, called for a ball of white thread. When this had been given him, he held up his hands with the palms together in the manner of salutation and blessed the thread. Then he solemnly drew four Yantras (cabalistic signs) on the papers prepared for them, and, handing these to his disciple together with the sacred thread and four light wooden posts, said to him: "Take these posts and set them up in the middle of the courtyard in the shape of a square. Then run the sacred thread round the four posts, and fold and put these Yantras on the thread, one between each two posts. When you have done this, unfold enough of the thread to place the ball in my hands." When the disciple had done as he was bid, the old priest ordered Meh Chan's father to bring the bowl of pure water and set it down on the ground in the centre of the square of sacred thread. "Take heed," said he, "and look closely into the water. There must not be one single speck of dust or dirt or impure matter in it, if you would see the buried figures when I call them into the bowl. If you are satisfied that the water is absolutely pure, place the snow-white cloth upon it and come away."

This act performed, the old priest lit one of the candles and gave it to the girl's father to fix upright on one side of the bowl, and then instructed him to have his daughter brought downstairs and laid beneath a little shelter which stood by the side of the courtyard near his prayer-mat, so that she might see all that was done.

When all things were ready, and the crowd alert with eager, curious eyes, the old priest, who was sitting about ten yards away from the bowl, held up the ball of thread with the palms of his hands together, and, closing his eyes, began to pray. As he sat thus in silent prayer, the girl's father and mother and all her friends, and also Meh Chan herself, regarded the old man with reverent eyes; and, even as they looked, some of his faith and trust began to steal its way into their hearts. They recognized at once that here was a much stronger, wiser man than any of the doctors or astrologers who had hitherto tried to cure Meh Chan. Their eyes wandered from the old priest's face to the bowl of water set within the sacred thread, and their hearts beat fast as they waited in sure expectation of the miracle that was about to happen. Meh Chan herself, although she could see but little, felt a spark of hope pass through her frame, and her face took on a faint tinge of colour. Such is the human trust in others' strength of mind.

For a long space of time the old priest prayed until the candle was half burnt down; then he opened his eyes, and calling the girl's family round him, said: "There is no shadow of doubt about it, she is under the spell of a sorcerer. He has buried figures of her and a man in the ashes of some cremated assassin, and there they lie on the funeral pyre in the heart of the virgin forest. But the evil influence that the sorcerer wields is so strong, and the image itself has lain so long, that, in spite of all my fervent prayer, I cannot call them up as yet. But have patience, and I will conquer in the end. Meanwhile prepare some food for your daughter to eat; I am sure she will be able to sit up and take some rice." And to the daughter: "Have no fear, my dear, but trust in me. You shall soon see the figures lying in the bowl."

These comforting words found a ready response in the sick girl's mind, and she began to take heart of grace; and when the rice was brought and set before her, she actually found it within her to eat a few of the separate, choicely cooked, ivory grains.

As soon as the priest had finished speaking, he shut his eyes once more, and continued in fervent, silent prayer until the candle had burnt completely out. Then he opened his eyes again and signed to the girl's father to go softly to the bowl and lift up the cloth. At this the whole company present rose to their feet and swayed forward in their eagerness to see. The father went to the bowl and lifted up the cloth, but at once cried out to the priest: "There is nothing in the bowl; I can see no figures." Then all the crowd fell back to their places, and a sigh of despair escaped their lips. Seeing that Meh Chan was sinking back to her former condition, the old priest turned to her and said: "How powerful this sorcerer is! But have no fear, however strong he may be, he must give way at last, for good will always overcome evil." So saying, he lit the second candle and gave it to his disciple to stick on the side of the bowl as before. The disciple received the candle and went inside the sacred thread, but in order to fix it on to the edge, he had to lift a corner of the cloth which covered the bowl, and in doing so found an easy means of slipping the waxen figures from under his nail into the pure, clear water. They slid to the bottom without a sound, and so adroitly and swiftly was the trick performed, that not a soul among those present was aware of it. Before putting the figures beneath his nail, the disciple had smeared them all over with ashes, and he stuck the candle so lightly on the edge that it only needed a gentle touch to make it fall into the bowl. Having rendered his service dutifully and reverently, he withdrew from the sacred thread and sat down behind his master once more.

The priest sat, as before, sunk in silent prayer, but before the candle was half burnt out the heat from the sun had warmed both the bowl and the candle, and the latter soon became soft. In a short while it was unable to bear its own weight, and, as it was stuck slightly towards the mouth of the bowl, presently it toppled over, fell on to the cloth, and, burning a hole, went through. All this time the old priest, who was pretending to keep his eyes shut tight, in reality was peeping through his half-closed lids and watching the candle closely; and as soon as he saw the candle fall in he gave a start, clutched the ball of thread, and pulled at the posts to which the thread was tied. As he pulled, the posts began to shake, and suddenly opening his eyes, he cried: "Now the figures have come, and with such force that they have knocked the candle over; you will find them all together lying at the bottom of the bowl."

This was the moment he had prayed for, for the people were so excited, and had seen the candle fall and the posts shake, and had heard the old priest cry out that the figures had come. With one accord they all surged forward, with Meh Chan's parents at their head; those in front tore off the remains of the cloth that covered the bowl, and there at the bottom they saw the figures and the candle-end lying side by side. It was true that the figures were very small, but the water was so pure and bright that they could see them as clear as daylight.

Meh Chan's father seized the figures and held them up for all to see, shouting out: "It's true, it's true, the figures have come; see them for yourselves." The company went almost delirious with joy; those behind who could not see started to press and fight to get a better place, and the sick girl herself, without another thought, stood up and tried to see over their heads, with trust and happiness written large all over her face.

Her father, pushing his way through the crowd, brought the figures for her to see, and then handed them to the priest, who carefully pointed out the marks of the ashes which they had received from the funeral pyre. Then the old man solemnly took a bottle of holy water and sprinkled it over Meh Chan, and made a circlet of sacred thread and placed it around her neck. The Yantras he ordered to be pasted on the walls of her bedroom, and turning to the young girl, said: "You see, my dear, I have not failed you. I have broken the spell of the sorcerer, and he has no power over you any more. Think of these terrible days as a dream that has gone; dismiss your fears, be happy, and marry the man you love."

Meh Chan smiled at him with her beautiful smile of olden time, and, falling at his feet, thanked him through her tears. Already her sickness was leaving her and she felt as one refreshed; indeed, she did not refuse a full bowl of rice which her mother brought her to soften the pangs of hunger already stealing through her body after her long fast. It was not long before her strength and spirits returned, and with them her beauty as of old. In due course her wedding day arrived, and with it the bridegroom she had made to wait until the spell was past.

NOTE BY PHYA MANUNET BANHĀN.—In this story we cannot help but praise the old priest, although he used deceit and guile; for he did it to gain a good end, and his reward was great.

If we must point a moral to adorn this tale, it shows us two things. First, how we must keep firm control over our mind in time of stress, and remember that whatever happens to us will of necessity be the result of our merit or lack of it. If we let go control and, so to speak, lose our reasoning powers, it is easily possible for such a state of mind to react on our bodies and make us, literally, seriously ill.

But secondly, on the other hand, how joy and pleasure and happiness, once aroused, are able to drive away all thought of disease, and thus the disease itself. So we should regard joy and happiness as one of the finest medicines and forms of sustenance that have ever been vouchsafed to us.

xi

THE STORY OF NAI PRASOP

"*Seek not to escape the mate whom Fate has ordained.*"
OLD SIAMESE PROVERB

LONG ago in Supanburi, about the middle of the fifteenth century, there lived the son of a wealthy old lady, who, to please his mother, had agreed to enter the priesthood. His name was Nai Prasop. When the appointed day arrived, his mother and their friends and relatives took him in their midst, clothed all in white, and went in procession to hand him over to the Head Priest of the temple he was about to enter, and to make a little merit on their own behalf.

Among those who joined the procession and followed in his mother's train was one of her female slaves, who, having a girl infant still suckling, took the child with her on her hip. When the procession arrived at the temple, as she did not wish to carry the child about, the slave placed a cradle under the cell that Nai Prasop was about to occupy and put the infant in it to sleep.

Now it happened that at the same time as Nai Prasop was initiated into the priesthood a certain astrologer of great repute among the townsfolk came to the temple to make merit for his sins, and when the ceremony of initiation was over and his folk had left him alone, Nai Prasop invited the astrologer into his cell, and asked him to consult his horoscope and reveal to him what his fate would be, especially the name of his future wife.

The astrologer complied, and, having made his calculations, told Nai Prasop three things: first, that his future bride would be the child of a slave; secondly, that she was still an infant; and thirdly, that at that very moment she was on a lower physical plane than he.

Having uttered these predictions, the astrologer took his leave.

Left to himself, Nai Prasop was very downcast and sore at heart at the thought that his wife was to be the child of a slave and not one of his own standing and position, but he accepted the omen without hesitation, for he had great faith in the astrologer's powers. As he lay brooding on these troublous thoughts he suddenly looked through a hole in the floor of his cell and observed the slave's infant lying on its back in a cradle fast asleep.

Seeing the child of his mother's slave lying directly beneath him, it came upon him with a sudden shock that here was the future bride predicted for him by the astrologer.

Then an evil thought came into his head, and he said to himself: "There can be no doubt about it: this is the infant to whom the astrologer referred. If I let her grow up to a marriageable age, his prediction will come true and I shall have to take her to wife. But I cannot and will not do it. I should be covered with shame, and could never look my own or my mother's friends in the face again. But now's my chance—the mother's away, and there's no one about. I must get rid of the child somehow while I can."

He was not really an evil-hearted boy, but his belief in the astrologer was strong, and opportunity is the lover of temptation. So, searching about, he found a house-knife used for cutting bamboo strips, and, inserting the blade in the hole in the floor just over the child's stomach, let the knife fall with a violent jerk of his hand. He thought the point would pierce the region of the infant's heart, but Fate decreed that the child's hour was not yet come. It happened that the knife swerved in falling and the shaft struck the side of the hole in the floor. So it missed the spot it was meant to strike, and the point of the knife entered the groin below the child's stomach instead. The wound it caused, although not fatal, was still a serious one, and the child set up such a scream of pain that its mother heard the noise at once and came rushing to see what had happened.

When she found the knife sticking in her child's groin and the child itself lying in a pool of blood, she was overcome with grief and anguish. She gave no heed then to who had done the deed, but plucked the knife from the wound and carried the child off as fast as she could go. Seeking out her mistress, she told her the story and showed her the child, and between them they washed and dressed the wound. Fortunately the infant was a healthy one, and the wound soon began to heal, and after some little time nothing was left but a scar to mark the spot.

Naturally the affair caused some little stir among the household, and it was not long before the slave found out the truth: that the son of her mistress was the author of the crime, and that he had tried to kill her child because an astrologer had predicted that she was to be his future bride. But even so, what could she do? She was only a slave, and she had no actual proof of his guilt. She could not go to her mistress with a tale of suspicion, and she therefore made up her mind that the only thing to do, as she could not bear to live near the son any more, was to try and discover some means of leaving the household. Luckily for her, she was able to find a friend to redeem her own and her husband's debts, and so she left the family, taking her husband and child with her; and from that time they disappeared as completely as if the earth had swallowed them up. Neither Nai Prasop nor his mother could find any trace of their whereabouts, in spite of all their diligent inquiry.

Now it happened that, some years after this, all the merit that the mother of Nai Prasop had acquired in the past spent its strength, and she fell on evil times. All her servants ran away and left her; her cattle, horses, and buffaloes died, her boats and rafts were lost, her wealth was gone, and there was nothing left for her in her old age but to lie down and die. The loss of his mother and wealth was a heavy blow to Nai Prasop. He had now no natural guardian, no one to look after his daily wants and supply him with his food, or candles, or betel. Although he was still in the priesthood, he began to feel his position acutely as he saw that the people around him no longer regarded him with the same favour as before. By becoming a priest he had brought merit to himself and his family, but now it was evident that he had no more merit within him, and he determined to retire from the priesthood and go into secular life. But when he came out into the world again there was nothing that he could do. He had never learnt a trade, and had no money with which to establish himself in any business. So he wandered about from place to place, looking for any kind of work which folk might give him out of kindness, to keep his body and soul alive. In the course of years he visited many towns and many villages, but never found a home in which to settle, until he happened one day, in a certain city, to enter the house of a rich merchant, to whom he offered himself as a servant. By chance the merchant had recently lost a servant and was seeking to replace him; and, as soon as he saw Nai Prasop, he liked the look of him.

It will be remembered that Nai Prasop was the son of wealthy parents, and although he had fallen low in the world, he had not forgotten his former estate, and still retained the breeding which his mother had taught him. His manners were good, and, finding the merchant willing to take him in, he resolved to do his utmost to serve and please him. So he entered the house as a servant, and, by his diligence and honesty and bearing, soon became a favourite of the family, so much so that after a certain time the daughter of the merchant fell in love with him, and he with her. When the parents of the girl discovered this, such was their regard for Nai Prasop that they raised no objection to the marriage, and at the proper season Nai Prasop and their daughter became man and wife amid great rejoicings.

They continued to live with her parents as before and were as happy as the day is long, until one night, when they had been married some little while, Nai Prasop noticed that his wife had a scar on her groin, as if she had been stabbed with a knife. At once his mind went back to the day of his terrible crime, for which he had suffered such remorse ever since; but, hiding his suspicions, he became sympathetic and loving towards his wife and tenderly asked her to tell him how it had happened and what was the cause.

His wife had, of course, heard the tale many times from her mother's lips, and this is the story she related to her husband: "Many years ago, dear, when I was very small, my father and mother were the slaves of an old lady who lived in Supanburi. On a certain day when the son of the old lady was to be initiated into the priesthood, my mother went with the procession to the temple, and, as I was still an infant, she took me with her as well, and put me into a cradle beneath the cell which the son would occupy as a priest. While I was asleep there, an astrologer came to visit the son in his cell and foretold that I was to be his future wife. In his disgust at such a thought, the son took a knife and tried to kill me, but by a happy accident the knife struck me in the groin and did not give me a mortal wound, and so I escaped and lived to become your wife, dear husband. But my father and mother refused to live any longer in the old lady's family, and, having found a friend to redeem them, left her and came to settle in this city. My father set up as a merchant, and by his honesty and ability has risen to the position in which you see him now."

Nai Prasop listened intently to his wife's tale, and almost at the first word recognized that she was the infant whom he had tried to kill. He thought to himself:

"By the Lord Buddha, to think that I was the son of a good family, that once my parents were people of wealth, which I imagined would last for ever. I never thought of this business of merit and demerit, which is able to change our lives in the twinkling of an eye, and which actually brought me down to a pretty low estate. And so I thought to escape my fate by killing the infant, who is now my wife. In those days she was on a lower plane than I, but on what a far lower plane am I now than she, and all through the merit and demerit we have earned! What a fool I was and a scoundrel!"

But he did not tell his thoughts to his wife.

NOTE BY PHYA MANUNET BANHĀN.—The moral of this story is clear. Whatever riches, honours, dignity we may possess, or whatever be our birth or pride of race, let us not bury it deep in our hearts. Fortune is a fickle jade and what we have to-day may be gone to-morrow. None of us know what the future holds.

But there is in Siamese a short poem which symbolizes the ideal union of man and woman:—

In our last incarnate state
You and I were man and mate—to death.
Tears we shared, and Treasure too;
Hearts we bared, whene'er we drew our breath.
All our countless lives adown
We have reaped what we have sown above.
Now, in this new glorious hour,
Bodies, hearts unite once more in love.

xii

THE FOUR JOLLY ROBBERS, OR THE PEPPER CURE

"*A little water will not extinguish a great fire.*"—OLD SIAMESE PROVERB

IN our grandfathers' time, so the story runs, there were four noted convicts who were serving heavy sentences for gang-robbery, but who managed to escape from prison and cleverly shook off all pursuit by donning the yellow robe in a country district in the heart of Siam, far away from the scene of their crime, having "gone to the Bodhi tree" for their initiation into the Order.[1] They pretended to be travelling priests seeking quiet and meditation in the jungle, and wandered about from one village to another. One day in the course of their travels they reached a deserted temple on the outskirts of a village, and finding the hall of worship still in pretty good repair, they adopted it as their place of refuge and entered in and lived there. They conducted themselves in such an orderly manner that the people of the village accepted them without demur as genuine priests, and soon came to have implicit trust in them. It pleased the simple folk to make merit by bringing them food and filling their bowls every morning.

Now one of this company of false priests was a good deal older than the others and was possessed of much wisdom and cunning, whereby he quickly assumed the position of spiritual teacher to all the people round about, and displayed considerable knowledge of the Mantras, as well as of the doctrines of the Buddhist religion. By this means he succeeded in deceiving the innocent peasantry so thoroughly that they came to

[1] A euphemistic way of saying that they were false priests.

regard him with great veneration and respect. In time he was regularly called upon to prepare holy water for them to sprinkle upon themselves and their houses, or else to bless the amulets which they concealed on their bodies to save them from pressing harms and dangers, and the old rogue never failed them. But he was not yet satisfied and wished to gain even greater respect, so he gave orders to the other three rascals to be ever on the watch for any of the villagers' animals that might go astray, whether horses, cattle, or buffaloes, and whenever they found one, to tie it up in a secret hiding-place in the jungle. Then, when the owner, having searched in vain, came to him for aid, and asked him to divine where his animal was, the old teacher would receive him in state, and, closing his eyes as if in the act of contemplation, would utter the following words: "Your animal still lives, and I know where it is hidden. Follow my directions closely, and you will surely find it again." With this he would give the villager minute directions as to the path he must follow, and in due course the latter would come to the place where the animal was hidden. He performed this miracle so many times that the villagers came to love him deeply and to pin their whole faith upon him. First they built him and his companions cells to live in; then they erected a substantial assembly hall, and finally they repaired the deserted temple and cleared and swept its precincts, so that, as you might say, it breathed out life again. But the four robber priests still conducted themselves in secret entirely contrary to the laws of the Order. They established an illicit still for making liquor, and showed little compunction in killing and eating by night the chickens, ducks, or pigs which the people set free in the temple grounds.

The villagers' kindness did not stop at building and repairing, but they brought presents of all the necessaries that a priest must have, fruit, betel, candles, pillows, and engaged themselves to be always at their command. Whatever the rascals demanded, whether goods or deeds, was at once supplied or performed by the villagers without delay. They did not know the evil characters of the guests they entertained so well.

In this way time slipped quickly by, until one day a thought occurred to the leader of the gang, and, calling his friends in secret council, he addressed them thus: "From the day we escaped from prison we have not enjoyed a single feast; what do you think of the idea of having a grand affair one evening?" And when the others had agreed with glistening eyes, he added: "But let us wait until a Holy Day occurs, and the villagers all come to make merit in the temple, and then leave it in my hands." To this the others willingly consented, and when the Holy Day arrived and the whole village was collected in the temple before him, the Head 'Priest' addressed them thus:—

" 'The reflection of the soul'[1] has recently made profound studies in astrology and divination, and from these studies it is clear that in seven days' time the 'spirit' of a deadly plague, accompanied by a swarm of satellites, is coming to visit this village. They will attack you in their hundreds. None of you will be able to stand up against them, and you will all be overwhelmed and die like rats caught in a trap. 'The reflection of the soul' would have no difficulty in escaping from the evil spirit's fatal clutch if he so wished, but his heart goes out to all you poor folk who will thus be left to die. You have been so kind and given such help to us that 'the reflec-

[1] This is a literal rendering of the priestly word for 'I' (Atmapāp) in which 'Atma' is the Sanskrit word for 'Soul', and 'Pāp' means a picture or reflection. To the Buddhist priest the world is illusion and nothing is abiding. Hence the term.

tion of the soul' has resolved to remain at his post and stand by you, and, if possible, to help you to escape from this awful calamity which is hanging over your heads."

When the villagers heard these words, young and old, men and maidens, one and all were stricken with panic and dismay. Many of them fell on their faces in the hall, and, crawling on their hands and feet towards the teacher, implored him to save their lives. Then the teacher comforted them and told them to be of good cheer. "I have a plan in my head," said he, "and if you will do as I tell you, I can save you. We must prepare a feast for the reception of this demon and his company of devils, and when we have lured them to eat the offerings inside the sacred thread, then they will be in my power, and I will bind them fast and destroy them. First, we must have a solemn ceremony in the Hall of Worship, and then I will enclose the boundaries of the temple grounds with the lines of sacred thread. For the offerings to be made, we must prepare two whole pigs' heads, and we must boil the bodies of fowls and ducks, ten of each. Next we must offer four sets of curry and rice with salad and all complete; then a huge jar of arrack, and not forget the tiers of banana leaves set to left and right. Last, sweetmeats and fruits there must be in profusion. When these have all been set in place, and the devils arrive at the appointed time, they will smell the feast prepared for them, and, urged on by greed, will enter within the sacred thread. Once within, they cannot escape and will be at my mercy. Thus you will escape the calamity which awaits you, and I shall have the satisfaction of knowing that I have been able to give you, in all humility of spirit, some genuine return for the many kindnesses you have showered upon us."

Then the villagers gathered their courage together,

and, taking heart, promised to make all things ready as the Head 'Priest' commanded them; and when the day of prophecy arrived, faithful to their promise, they came to the temple laden with curry and rice, fowls and ducks, the heads of pigs, sweetmeats and fruits, jars of arrack, and tiers of banana leaves to garnish the feast. Then the Head 'Priest' told the elders of the village to summon all the people to the Temple Hall to hear his further commands, and when the villagers were assembled, he addressed them again: "Kind friends all, listen to my words. To-night is the fateful night, when the King of the Plague and his company of demons will come to attack you. I and my fellow priests will now place the sacred thread round the temple precincts, and for three full days we must pray and fast before we can overcome and destroy these devils. You must all go back to your homes and shut yourselves in, and offer up constant prayers to be protected from all evil. Until we have subdued them, the power of these devils is still very strong, and if any of you so much as dares to enter within the sacred thread during these three days, he will assuredly become stark, raving mad. Therefore beware, my brethren, and take heed. Bitter is the battle we have to fight: we need all your faith and obedience."

Then the Head 'Priest', aided by his fellows, with solemn rites set the feast in place, and encircled the temple's limits with the sacred thread; and, having done so, dismissed the village folk to their homes with his blessing. No sooner had they all departed, than the Head 'Priest' called the other three, and, going once more into the Hall of Worship, gave forth peal after peal of shouts. As the noise of the shouts echoed and re-echoed through the silent hall, it reached the villagers' ears, and struck their fear-ridden hearts as the cries of a hundred demons. They were sure that the devils had arrived, and, closing their ears with their hands, feverishly hurried back to their homes.

When they arrived, so thoroughly imbued were they all with trust in the 'priest' and fear of the devils, that they hastily pulled up the outer steps of their houses, closed and bolted the doors and windows, put out all their lights, and sank on their knees in prayer, even as their teacher had commanded them. Once entrenched, not a living soul dared to set his foot outside his own threshold.

When the 'priests' were satisfied that they were absolutely alone, with laughs and quips they hungrily sat themselves down to the feast, and in a short space of time were enjoying the delights of roasted duck and pig's head, boiled chicken and rice and curry of fresh prawns, with chillies and all kinds of salads, washed down with draughts of fermented liquor. As the feast progressed, they began to shout and sing. One of them rose and danced to the lilt of a song; the others recounted with mock seriousness the stories of their past crimes, and laughed to themselves at the easy way in which they had fooled the villagers—all in the cherished belief that they were completely safe from prying eyes.

Now it so happened that, some time before the week of warning and preparation, one of the villagers, named Nai Wang Dee, who was more or less a new-comer, had gone on a visit to his relatives in another village some distance away, and had not yet returned. Thus he knew nothing of the 'priest's' prophecy, or of the trick that had been played upon his fellow-villagers. But Nai Wang Dee chose the very night of the feast to return home, and his easiest path, as he neared the village, led him through the grounds of the robbers' temple. As he approached, completely unaware of the lines of sacred thread, he just passed underneath them and went on his way through the garden. But when Nai Wang Dee came opposite the Hall of Worship, he at once became aware of a noise proceeding from it, and one can imagine his surprise and fright when he heard the shouts and ribald laughter of drunken men. Turning round to look at the new quarters which had been built for the 'priests', he saw that they were all in darkness, and, his suspicions being slightly aroused, he went up close to the entrance to the Hall and peered through a chink in the door. There he saw a dreadful sight. All the four 'priests', their robes thrown aside, sitting, lying, dancing, eating, and drinking in every kind of drunken pose. As he listened intently, he could hear them telling in detail, with all their rascally zest, how they had spent their early years in robbing, raping, and every kind of crime, and cracking their sides with laughter at the thought of how they had fooled the simple villagers. At first he stood aghast, dumbfounded, unable to think or act. But when it dawned upon him fully that these four drunken ruffians were the saintly 'priests' they had housed and clothed and fed, his gorge rose within him, and, collecting his scattered senses, he thought hard of what might best be done. Unarmed as he was, it was useless for him to attempt to deal with them alone, and if he raised the alarm then and there, he was certain they would not scruple to attack him at once. He made up his mind that the only thing to do was to rouse the whole village, and, when they understood how they had been tricked, he felt sure they would join him in a concerted attack upon the robbers. So, stepping gently down the steps of the Assembly Hall, Nai Wang Dee sped away home as fast as he could go. When he arrived, he saw, to his astonishment, that not only his own but all the doors around were shut, the steps drawn up, and the lights extinguished, and he could hear the sound of people praying hard. As he could think of no possible reason to account for this, he called out in a loud voice: "Ho! Ho! What is the meaning of this? Why are you praying behind closed doors with all the lights out? You know those four 'priests' we have fed and housed so long. Well, I have just found out that they are now at this moment having a feast in the temple, singing, dancing, and drinking away to their hearts' content. Come out, all of you, and help me attack them, and when we have captured them, we'll march them off to the Governor of the Province."

At first, when the villagers heard Nai Wang Dee's cries, they thought the demons had escaped from the temple and had come to devour them. In their fear they fell flat on their faces and lay absolutely still, listening to every sound. But in a short time they recognized Nai Wang Dee's voice, and this gave them a start, for most of them had entirely forgotten his very existence. From his words it was clear that, on his way back from his own village, he must have taken the path through the temple grounds, and, all unwittingly, gone inside the sacred thread. There was no doubt about it, he must be mad. So his wife, with her father and mother and relatives, opened the door, and, rushing down the steps, which they hastily replaced in a panic, seized hold of Nai Wang Dee. But the more they held him, the more angry he became, and he kept on shouting out: "I am not mad, but in perfect possession of all my senses. But I have seen those four rascals, whom we thought were priests, eating and drinking at this very moment in the temple, and they're all hopelessly drunk. I tell you I peeped through a chink in the door and saw them all clearly. If you don't believe me, come with me and see for yourselves."

But it was no use; not a soul would listen to him. The more he shouted and the more excited he became, the more they thought he was beside himself and mad. So they all rushed at him, and, seizing him violently, bound him with ropes and locked him up in a room in his house. Left to himself, Nai Wang Dee's heart began to fail him, as he thought: "What's the use of anything? I come home and tell them the truth, and all I receive in return is that they lock me up and say I am mad."

At a later hour the elders of the house visited him, and, seeing him now quite quiet, said to one another: "This is the man we used to know, honest and straight-speaking as he always was." But as soon as he began to repeat to them the same story and to demand of them to accompany him to the scene as witnesses, they regretfully shook their heads and agreed that he must be mad. The fact was that the whole village was in such a state of terror that he could never have found a single person to believe him, however hard he had tried. So they shut him up and kept him behind locked doors until the full three days were up. On the morning following the third day a council of the chief villagers was called at Nai Wang Dee's house, and after an earnest consultation, it was finally decided that the best thing to do was to take Nai Wang Dee in a body to the temple and ask the priests to cure him. They would explain what had happened, and how Nai Wang Dee had come by chance within the sacred thread, entirely in ignorance and without any intent to disobey the Head 'Priest'. No sooner decided, than done. Along they went, with the whole village behind them, and with Nai Wang Dee still bound in their midst, and when they reached the temple, they found the four 'priests' at their work as usual, the Head 'Priest' studiously reading, with another by his side, another mending the spokes of his umbrella and another sweeping the floor, for they had no acolytes to help them.

The Head 'Priest' received them kindly, and, having heard the cause of their visit and the explanation they gave of Nai Wang Dee's conduct, gravely said: "A cure must be found, if it can, for to cast aside a man who is mad is to lose a living soul. I have a remedy at hand, and will do my best to help both him and you. But it is a powerful remedy, and first of all I require six strong young men to hold the patient down on his back."

At these words Nai Wang Dee's anger knew no bounds, and, lifting up his voice and pointing at the 'priests,' he cried: "There they are, the damnable villains, setting themselves up as priests, but eating and drinking in the temple like the rogues and ruffians they are, and now pretending to cure me of madness!" But the Head 'Priest' appeared to take no notice, beyond a smile at the villagers, and picked out six strong young men, who at once came forward, seized hold of Nai Wang Dee and laid him down on the ground on the flat of his back. Then the Head 'Priest' went into his cell and prepared two doses of pepper in two short bamboo tubes. With one in each hand he approached the patient, and saying, "This is splendid stuff for a violent gall," he blew the pepper up his nose, one up each nostril. When he received the full force of the pepper, Nai Wang Dee nearly went off his head. He struggled and shouted, and went on exhausting himself until he nearly fainted with anger and pepper. Meanwhile the Head 'Priest' quietly left the assembly and went and prepared two more tubes of pepper; and, coming forth again, said: "This remedy of mine is, as I have said, a very strong one, and as a rule one dose suffices. If it doesn't cure him soon, I will try another dose; but if that fails too, it will be a sure sign that he cannot be cured at all." He spoke this quietly, and yet so clearly and firmly that it took hold of the mind of Nai Wang Dee; and when he saw the

Head 'Priest' advancing with another dose of pepper in each hand, he realized that the game was up, and that it was useless for him to try and fight the rascals single-handed, with all his own folk against him. The only result, if he continued the fight, would be another dose of pepper, and possibly death at the end, and he could not see himself becoming a martyr for a thousand such rogues as these. So he made up his mind to give in, and, suddenly rising up as if out of sleep, said, as he looked around him: "What is all this? Why am I lying here bound with ropes? Why do you all stare at me so?" And when he saw the Head 'Priest,' he made obeisance and offered him every mark of respect, and said to him: "It is a strange thing, you know. I feel as if I had been asleep and had a very singular dream. I dreamt that I was passing a temple door, and looking inside I saw a company of devils dressed as priests eating and drinking and making merry. As I stood horror-struck at the sight, I suddenly lost my senses and I knew no more. I thank the Lord Buddha that I have now regained my senses and can shake off the effects of this evil dream." Then his family and all the folk gathered round him and patted him on the back and said: "Now you're much better, but what a lucky escape you have had, and how kind the Head 'Priest' has been to cure you; you must thank him properly, for it is entirely due to him that you are not still a madman." So the wretched fellow, having thanked the Head 'Priest' (not without gnashing of teeth), was led away home by his folk. But when he found himself in his wife's home once more, all his anger rose up within him again as he thought of how he had been treated by the robbers, and how his wife and her family all put their implicit trust in the four rascals, and had refused to believe him, even going to the length of putting ropes upon him and locking him up in his own house. The thought that he had been forced to tell lies for seemingly no reason at all made him very sore at heart, and he said to himself: "If all the others disbelieve me, I am sure my wife loves me and will listen to what I have to say." So when they went to bed that night he began to whisper earnestly to his wife: "Sweetheart, I only told you the truth about those priests. I saw them with my own eyes having a drunken orgy in the temple, and I heard them with my own ears recounting the story of their crimes and of how they had escaped from prison. I honestly saw them, and if you don't believe me when I tell you now, when will you ever do so?"

But when this wife heard Nai Wang Dee talking in this manner, she thought to herself: "By the Lord Buddha, he is going mad again, what on earth shall I do?" So she jumped out of bed and rushed off to her father and mother, bursting in upon them, saying: "My husband has gone raving mad again, you must come and help me with him!" Then Nai Wang Dee realized that even his wife had no faith in him, and his heart sank to its lowest depths, the more so as he saw in his imagination the pepper cure applied again. He thought to himself: "This is no place for me—as long as I live among these idiotic folk I shall be the only one to suffer." So he too leapt up from the bed and ran out of the house, and shaking its dust from off his feet, made straight for his own village and home.

NOTE BY PHYA MANUNET BANHĀN.—This story is an excellent example of the old sayings, "A little water will not extinguish a great fire", or, "If you live among folk whose eyes are closed, you had better close yours as well".

It serves to remind us that, although we may be speaking the truth and actually thereby conferring a great benefit on others, if our words do not coincide with the thoughts and desires of those we are trying to serve, no advantage will accrue either to the speaker or to the listener. Indeed, it may well happen that disaster will overtake the speaker, even as in this tale. The wish is father to the thought.

xiii

THE EFFECT OF TRUTH, OR THE FARMER'S DILEMMA

SOME twenty or thirty years ago there were living on the bank of a 'klong' near Supanburi a young Siamese and his wife, who were farmers. They had been eagerly awaiting the arrival of a child for some little time, when suddenly in the middle of the night, a short while before it was due, the wife was seized with violent pains, and they knew that the hour had come.

As the nearest midwife lived in the village two or three miles away, the husband became very alarmed in his mind. There were only two or three other families living near by, and all he could think of was to call in their women-folk to help. They came at once at his request and did all that they could to ease the wife's travail, and eventually the child was safely delivered, to the husband's great joy and pride. But, unfortunately, the wife still continued in great pain, and, in spite of all their united efforts, not only by giving her holy water to drink but also by pressing and squeezing her violently, they could not bring her relief. At last her condition became critical and she gradually began to sink. There was no trained nurse among them, and all that those present could do was to sit and dumbly watch the patient's eyes, fearing the worst, but hoping for the best. At length the husband could bear the strain and anxiety no longer in silence, and, casting round in his mind for other possible means of help, bethought him of a priest who some days before had moored his boat to the landing-place in front of his house. He said to the others, who also knew of the priest's presence: "I have filled his bowl for three days running; I will go and ask him to come and have a look at my wife. He might be able to do something for her. After all, he's a priest, and even if he only pronounces two or three magic words over her, that will be worth more than all we farmers can do put together." So off he went down to the priest's boat and begged him to come and help his wife. But the priest shook his head and said: "I'm afraid it's no good asking me, I have no charms or incantations to fit such a case as this." The husband wrung his hands in despair, and cried: "There is literally nobody else who can help her. By all the spirits of Earth and Heaven, come before it is too late and befriend us now in our time of need." The priest could resist his entreaties no longer, and, remembering how the husband had daily filled his bowl, finally consented to go with him. Seeing the woman in a sinking condition, he thought of all the charms and incantations of which he had ever heard and repeated them over her. He gave her holy water to drink, while the husband shook her head violently to and fro. Still there was no change in the wife's condition, and in the end he also could do nothing but, like the rest, sit and watch her slowly fading away. Realizing at length that the woman would probably die if nothing further was done, the priest reflected for a few moments, and then, turning suddenly to the husband, said: "An end to charms and sprinklings! Of what possible use are they at a time like this? No, we must try other and better means. We three, I and you and your wife, must each earnestly resolve to confess, now and openly to one another, the most heinous sin that we have ever committed and have kept secret from one another, and, having done so, we must all solemnly promise that never again will we commit this sin, calling upon the Three Gems and our Guardian Spirits to protect us and keep us true to our promise given. One cannot say, but perhaps the force of the truth we utter may be strong enough to bring your wife relief."

Being at the end of their resources, and seeing no other help at hand, the husband and wife somewhat falteringly agreed. First of all, the husband asked all the neighbours present to leave the house. When they had gone, the priest placed a bowl of holy water between them and stuck a lighted candle on the rim of the bowl; and then, all things being ready, the three of them began to call on the Buddha, the Law, and the Order, and to pray to all their Guardian Spirits, down to the Spirit of the House, to aid them in their task.

As the priest had been the originator of the idea, the husband suggested that he should be the first to begin. Whereupon the priest opened his heart and confessed: "I am no true priest, but a robber, who have many times suffered imprisonment. But I escaped and stole these yellow robes, and the reason of my coming here was to rob you all when you had gone to sleep. I solemnly swear that I will never commit a robbery again."

Next the husband, with nervous eyes upon his wife, said as firmly as he could: "For the last three months that my wife has been expecting a child I have been committing adultery with her younger sister, and I actually had made up my mind to elope with her. I solemnly swear that I will commit adultery no more."

This roused the wife as perhaps nothing else could have done, and, raising herself on her elbow, she cried at him. "You vile wretch! so that's what you've been doing these last three months. Well, learn now from your wife's lips that this is no child of yours!" Then, sinking back on to her mat once again, she repeated the formula; "I solemnly swear that I will commit adultery no more."

As soon as the three had confessed their sins and had taken their solemn oaths to commit them no more, the robber-priest took the candle and dropped it into the bowl of holy water, and as he did so he raised his folded hands and cried: "May the strength of the truth we have spoken and of the oaths we have taken, in confessing our sins and in solemnly promising to commit them no more, give to this holy water in the bowl the magic power to bring this woman relief from her labour now and at once."

Then he took the bowl of water and, sprinkling some of it on her head and stomach, gave her the rest to drink; and such was the virtue of their united power that the wife's pains ceased from that hour.

xiv

THE MISSING ELEMENT

"One must use a thorn to draw a thorn."—OLD SIAMESE PROVERB

IN the reign of King Narai there lived near Ayudhya a married couple named Nai Hah Tong and Nang Song Sai, who were people of substance and property, but not to the extent of riches. Now Nang Song Sai was an intelligent, industrious soul, and an excellent, practical housewife, so that, if her husband had sought his living, as most other folk in this world, in some well-ordered and established branch of business, there was nothing to prevent him becoming in time an honoured and prosperous citizen. But Nai Hah Tong did not conduct himself or seek his livelihood like other normal men; on the contrary, ever since he took Nang Song Sai to wife, he had spent the whole of his time in studying alchemy, and in seeking recipes for the transmutation of metals, to the end that he might change base, reddish copper into pure, shining, yellow gold. This he had done for a number of years, yet without a shadow of success. But although his patience, in spite of his trials, was not yet at an end, his own means and those of his wife began to show signs of exhaustion in this absorbing game of alchemy. At length his wife became alarmed, and expostulated with her husband not only on the utter futility of his efforts, but also on his almost criminal negligence in thus wasting their substance; but all to no purpose, for Nai Hah Tong declined to listen to her, and only said that she must have patience, even as he. In her despair at length she sought out her father, and poured out the story of her husband's maddening conduct into his sympathetic ears. Her father listened without saying a word, but, when his daughter had left him, he sent a servant to ask his son-in-law to come and pay him a visit. Nai Hah Tong at once set out and on his arrival, after the customary greetings, the old man addressed him this:

"I hear that you are much interested in alchemy and have been carrying on experiments for a long time past, but, although you have had no success as yet, you have never thought of consulting me in this difficult matter. Perhaps you think that I have no knowledge of the subject, but I would have you know that I have long practised this art and have dived deep into its secrets. Indeed, I know the recipe of a certain solution which, if used to wash copper, can turn it into 'nopakhun'[1] gold in the twinkling of an eye. But now I am an old man and have had to give up the task, for the preparation of this solution requires years of patient toil."

Nai Hah Tong gazed at his father-in-law almost with adoration in his eyes, for he saw already in his imagination his long cherished desire being brought to fruition at last. So he closed the palms of his hands together and, raising them in token of veneration and respect, replied:

"Dear father-in-law, I pray you tell me the nature of this solution; even if it takes years and years to prepare, I will 'clench my teeth' until I have succeeded in producing it, for I have struggled now for many years and all in vain."

The old man, seeing that his son-in-law believed his words and had faith in him, thereupon continued:

"All the elements necessary for the preparation of this solution are at hand in my house except one. It is this one that you must seek and use all your endeavours

[1] 'Nophakun' is the ninth quality, or the purest gold.

to obtain, and yet it is by no means difficult to acquire. Whether you find it or not depends entirely on your own skill and labour. The element that I need is the white powdery down to be found on banana leaves, and this I must have to the weight of two 'catties'.[1] Yet you must not think that you can collect this down from the banana-trees of other folk. No, the trees must be your own, and the planting of every tree and the digging of every hole must be accompanied by incantations solemnly repeated by yourself. The sooner you desire to obtain the required amount of down, the more banana-trees you will naturally have to plant; and if you find any difficulty in procuring sufficient capital for the enterprise, I will do my best to come to your aid and supply whatever is lacking."

By this time Nai Hah Tong was almost beside himself with joy, so bitten was he in his search for gold, and he knew that his own substance had sadly dwindled during the years of his past experiments; and when he returned home and told his wife of the advice which her father had given him and of his promise to help them, she was equally delighted and agreed to do her utmost to make the scheme a success.

And now a period of great activity set in. All the available capital that the couple could procure, as well as that provided by the wife's father, was laid out in the purchase of land, in hiring labour to clear it, and finally in turning it into plantations of bananas; no time indeed was lost in putting into action the advice given by the old man. But once the trees were planted under his supervision, Nai Hah Tong took no thought of how many 'rai'[2] of bananas they planted, or of how many trees went to the 'rai'. As soon as the trees were grown, his whole attention was absorbed in finding

[1] A 'catty' is equal to $1\frac{1}{3}$ lbs.

[2] 5 rai = 2 acres.

which trees and how many leaves could provide him with the powdery down his heart desired, and when he had collected his daily measure, he weighed it with the utmost care and scruple to see how the store was increasing. On the other hand, his industrious wife spent her whole day in supervising the work of the plantations, in examining the trees, in carefully selecting the bunches of bananas to be cut, and in offering them for sale, both fresh and sun-dried.

In this manner three years passed by, and it was not long before the couple had gained a high reputation in the neighbourhood as the owners of large and well-managed banana plantations. The front of their house, which bordered the river, became one of the most important wharves in the district for the purchase and sale of bananas. At all hours of the day and night numbers of boats might be seen collected in the river with prospective purchasers on board, but still Nai Hah Tong did not bother his head to ask what all this bustle meant, or what kind of a trade they were doing in bananas. Every morning of his life he rose up early and went into the plantations to see that the labourers were tending the stems as carefully as possible, so that they should grow into handsome trees and produce fine, long leaves, with a large amount of down. And every evening he gathered his collection of down and weighed it carefully on his arrival home. Thus two more years slipped by, and at length, after five years of strenuous endeavour, he had obtained the two 'catties' of down that his father-in-law required.

Believing that the dream of his life was about to come true, he seized his precious load and rushed off to find the old man. With trembling hands and glowing eyes he showed him the two 'catties'of down, and cried: "At last I have the missing element, and we can begin our experiments at once." But his father-in-law only laughed and said: "Yes, you are going to be a rich man now."

At this Nai Hah Tong went almost mad with joy; his countenance flushed, and he shook so much with excitement that he could scarcely keep still.

Then the old man, without further words, sent a servant to summon his daughter to him, and when she arrived, he asked her if she had made any money recently by selling bananas. On her replying that she had done so, he said to her: "Bring it all here for me to see."

Hearing his father-in-law speak in this fashion, Nai Hah Tong became a little suspicious in his mind, and sat confused, wondering what connection money gained from the sale of bananas had with the transmutation of metals, and what possible use it could be to them in their experiments; but he said nothing, for his heart was still full of the thought that at last he had the missing element.

In a short while Nang Song Sai came back, and counted out before his astonished eyes all the profit she had gained by selling bananas and the stems of the trees during the past five years, to the extent of not less than twenty thousand ticals.

As soon as Nang Song Sai had finished her counting, the old man turned to Nai Hah Tong and said:

"Look at the money that you have made out of my recipe for changing metals! Now, if you want to turn this money into gold of the seventh, eighth, or ninth quality, or, if you prefer it, into diamonds and sapphires, or into elephants, horses, cows, and buffaloes, or even into silken robes, why, you can choose whichever you like. To my mind, mine is a much better recipe than any of those that you have been studying all these years."

The old man finished speaking, but Nai Hah Tong remained dumb, unable to utter a single word, because it had only just dawned upon him that his wife had been making all this money by selling bananas. On the one hand, he was naturally pleased to find that they had made so much profit from their banana plantations; on the other hand, his heart was sore that his father-in-law had deceived him. For some time chagrin and pleasure struggled together for mastery in his mind, but at length pleasure gained the upper hand, and he allowed a smiling ray to pass over his face. Then the old man gave him the following words of counsel:

"You ought to know that this game which you have been indulging in of trying to change copper or lead or silver into pure shining gold is against the law of Nature, is against the very nature of the minerals themselves. The substance of minerals is a thing which arises of itself deep in the earth through the age-long action of heat and cold, and in no sense through the action of man. Do you think for a moment that we, poor humans, can change the substance of minerals in the same way as we can dye a piece of cloth? We human beings have a spirit within us and are animate, knowing well the difference between good and evil. Even so, it is no easy task to reform an evil man and teach him to be good. How then do you imagine that we can succeed in changing the substance of some inanimate object? It is clear that we must abandon all hope of changing one element into another. But with other occupations, such as planting bananas, there is every hope of assured success. Look back, young man, and recall the period when you were playing at your alchemy, before you took up the planting of bananas, how much profit did you get out of it? None at all, but only loss. But if you think of the last five years, up to this present time, you have gained a profit of twenty thousand ticals, and in the future your prosperity will increase according to the condition of your plantations and to the ability and energy which you employ in their care. Stick to bananas, my boy, and leave alchemy alone."

Nai Hah Tong listened to the old man's words, and his heart grieved for all the time he had wasted and all the losses he had suffered in playing with metals. He saw clearly the benefit he had derived from the trick which had been played upon him in making him plant bananas, and from that time onwards he gave up all his attempts at alchemy and devoted himself to work.

Indeed, to show his gratitude, he took his collection of down, and, having mixed it with rice water, fashioned a figure of his father-in-law; and when he died he gave it to his family as a heirloom in memory of the old man's kindness.

NOTE BY PHYA MANUNET BANHĀN.—In this story we cannot but admire the trick played by the wise old man, which agrees so fittingly with the ancient proverb, "One must use a thorn to draw a thorn." If the father-in-law had not used a recipe for the transmutation of metals, a subject dear to the heart of Nai Hah Tong, as a cloak for hiding his stratagem, however earnestly he had counselled his son-in-law, the latter would never have been able to see the error of his ways.

XV

THE DROP OF HONEY

ONCE upon a time, long, long ago, there reigned in a certain village peace, contentment, and happiness. No man's hand was raised against his neighbour, and innocent simplicity vied with rustic kindliness in the villagers' daily life.

But one day there entered that village a stranger bearing on his shoulders a load of wild honey, gathered from the hives of the silver-smooth bee-trees which grow along the path of the country-side, and from that load of honey one drop fell to earth. A gecko [1] saw it, and crept to lick it up. A cat espied the lizard and ran to seize it in its mouth. A dog leapt out and bit the cat. The owner of the cat, who was standing by, was enraged at the dog and beat it with a stick. The dog's howling brought its master out to see what caused the noise. At the sight of his dog being beaten, he dashed forward and kicked the owner of the cat. The owner of the cat retaliated, and a battle royal ensued between the two. The noise of the fight grew louder and louder until, a hue and cry being raised, the family and friends of the owner of the cat gathered together and came to his aid against the owner of the dog. At once, however, the relations and friends of the owner of the dog became aware of the fight, and they in their turn came to his assistance against the owner of the cat. In a short space of time —in almost less time that it takes to tell—the inhabitants had divided themselves into two camps, the one to fight for the owner of the dog, the other to fight for the owner of the cat, and both sides rushing into the fray, the whole village became one wild shouting tumult. At first the

[1] A small lizard, to be seen on the walls of all houses in Further India.

villagers contented themselves with using their feet, their fists, and their teeth, but as the fight became more furious, and both sides ever more bold, some seized sticks, and others stones, until at length one grasped his ancient muzzle-loading gun and fired it. Each side then realized that a war had started in earnest, and began to entrench itself within its camp, digging by day and digging by night. Sallies were made and raids on the opposing camps, even as in an actual state of war, and soon the dividing stretch of land between was strewn with the dead and wounded. Matters having reached this state, and neither party being able to gain much advantage, each side became more and more determined to conquer the other. Both therefore sent out calls to the villages near by, imploring them to come to their help in the struggle. So serious did it at last become that, news being brought to the capital, the King had to order out the soldiery, and it needed a large troop to be led into action and the loss of a number of lives before the district could be subdued, and order and peace brought at last into the village once again.

And the cause of all this trouble was a single drop of honey.

Note by Phya Manunet Banhān.—This story shows us clearly that the force of anger, like a forest fire, if one has not sufficient sense to stamp it out at once, is likely to spread until it becomes a calamity of the direst kind. Thus it serves to remind and admonish us to try our utmost to suppress, at its very outset, any cause of quarrel which may arise while yet it has but little power. If we do not exercise our judgment and reason at such a time, then we must bear the full force of the raging flame to which such a quarrel may lead, as in this tale of the single drop of honey.

REFLECTIONS

I

DURING the past half-century a considerable number of books on Siam have been produced by various authors, including myself, which are well known to people who have a definite interest in the country; and yet, when all is said, there is no book in English within my knowledge that allows the Siamese to speak for himself, that will show you at first hand how his mind works, what is his capacity for humour, or what his outlook on life. All the books on Siam that I have read are but interpretations of that mind and of that outlook seen through Western eyes and dressed in Western garb.

I hear it sometimes said that the Siamese have no literature to speak of, and that the Siamese language is not worth studying deeply for that reason. From the European point of view, with its own criterion of literature, there is, I suppose, some truth in the allegation. The Siamese have not yet reached the stage of novel-writing, which, after all, is of comparatively modern growth among ourselves, though foreign novels are now being freely translated into Siamese, Conan Doyle and Rider Haggard being great favourites. Sometimes, too, European stories are adapted in translation to suit the Siamese taste. Nor have they evolved any such form of literature as essay-writing. Most of their prose literature deals with religious subjects, and there are no great prose classics. Even the famous *Sam Kok* is a translation of Chinese history. But very few Europeans have ever attempted to study Siamese at all seriously, much less to take any deep dive into Siamese poetry, which is in its own way highly developed, and is their most natural form of expression in secular literature. It is, perhaps, more dependent on the niceties of rhyming and the euphony of its language, than on the beauty of the ideas underlying it or on its appeal to the soul of man. But that these ideas are by no means lacking may be clearly seen from the short poem given at the end of "The Story of Nai Prasop".

Siamese poetry is divided into many kinds, such as 'Kam Klawn', the metre of the famous 'Khun Chang Khun Paen', 'Kam Klong', and 'Kam Chan', which is a high form of a very difficult nature. No one has yet attacked the subject of Siamese poetry seriously in a foreign language, and Siamese thought will never be understood in the West until their poetry is fully explained.

As for the stories I have told in this volume, whether they are to be reckoned as great literature or not, I will maintain that no one having read them will deny to the Siamese a capacity for the short story, and a sense either of humour or of the drama. There is a terseness and a directness about them, a relish and a flavour, which must make an appeal to the receptive mind.

It would seem that, in the development of their natural attributes, the Siamese, that is, the bulk of the people who are peasants, are at the present time somewhat at the stage which Northern Europe had reached in the Middle Ages. The country has not been peacefully settled long enough for any great development in education to have taken place, but the people, being of a free and independent turn of mind, have a lively sense of humour, somewhat broad, of a Chaucerian kind, as I have said in the preface, and their thoughts are mostly tinged with religion, or at any rate with fears of the natural and supernatural phenomena all around them. Magic, both sympathetic and contagious, still plays a great part in their lives, and their ears and eyes are open to every wind that blows, every bird that calls, and every leaf that rustles in the mysterious, enchanted forest. Nowadays the townsfolk are becoming more sophisticated, through their schools and contact with Western ideas, but the great mass of the people still remains untouched, and the peasants are a hardy, lovable race, rooted to the soil they till. It is remarkable how all the oppression and all the tyranny of the past centuries have left them still free and uncomplaining. I have been often among them, sat with them at their village councils, and marvelled at their independence of thought and bearing, their patience, and their responsive, sidelong glances at any glimpse of humour. Trust them as a friend, as an equal, and they will open their hearts. Come among them as an official with stern, unbending mien, and they will close their mouths like oysters at the touch.

The Siamese have an almost inexhaustible fund of proverbs, wonderfully incisive and penetrating, as you will have seen from the stories themselves, going straight to the core of things, and leaving little room for doubt as to their knowledge of the realities of life. One they have which takes us back to Burns's famous couplet, and which runs like this: "We look at others with our front eyes, but we see ourselves with those behind."

This is not the proverb of a young race. It speaks of thousands of years of knowledge and experience of the game of life, and in fact the Siamese are not a young race, although they have scarcely been a thousand years in what is now Siam, in the same way as we English can barely count a thousand years of history in our present home. In truth, the Siamese or Thai, as they call themselves, come of an ancient Pamir plateau stock, which settled in Southern China several thousand years ago, and the accumulated lore which is now ours for the seeking has been handed down to the modern Siamese by their ancestors of long, long ago.

Consider the tenth story in this book, "The Buried Figures". If we look deep enough, it is easy to see that the moral of the story applies to mankind at all times and in all places. What is the story but an example of auto-suggestion, which is as rife among Europeans as it is among Eastern folk? I have known an Englishman in Siam make himself seriously ill, so ill as to be compelled to resign his official position, largely through studying a medical book on diseases.

Look at the old priest's knowledge of the value of a setting. Could one better his choice of the ashes of a cremated assassin in the heart of the virgin jungle from which to call up the buried figures? And then again, the efficacy of magic. Most educated people, reading the story of the old priest's ruse, would think the village folk almost unbelievably simple and credulous. But anyone who has read the first four chapters of the famous *Golden Bough* by Sir James Frazer will know how little removed the mass of Europeans are from this same belief in the efficacy of magic.

Here are two examples of sympathetic magic recorded within recent years in England itself.

In Sussex some fifty years ago a maid-servant strongly opposed the throwing away of children's cast teeth, affirming that if such a tooth happened to be found and gnawed by an animal, the child's new tooth would be exactly like that of the animal in question. In proof she quoted old Master Simmons who had a large pig's tooth in his upper jaw, because, according to him, his mother had thrown one of his cast teeth by accident into a pig's trough.

In Suffolk, if a man runs a thorn or, as he calls it,

a bush into his hand, he oils or greases the extracted thorn. For example, a farmer came to a doctor not long ago with an inflamed hand, having run a large thorn into it. On being told that the hand was festering, he replied: "That didn't ought to, for I greased the bush well after I pulled it out." Similarly in Cambridgeshire, if a horse runs a nail into its foot, or, as in one case, hurts its side on the hinge of a farm gatepost, nothing is done to the horse, but the nail or the hinge is taken out, well greased and put away, because this will bring about the recovery of the animal.

Here is a recipe, quoted by Sir Francis Bacon as a remedy for cuts or sores or wounds, which shows the antiquity of this remedy:—

"It is constantly received and asserted", says Bacon, "that the anointing of the weapon which maketh the wound will heal the wound itself. In this experiment, upon the relation of men of credit (though myself, as yet, am not fully inclined to believe it), you shall note the points following: First the ointment wherewith this is done is made of divers ingredients, whereof the strongest and hardest to come by are the moss upon the skull of a dead man unburied, and the fats of a boar and a bear killed in the act of generation."

If these ingredients were absolutely essential to the experiment, then I should say that it was very rarely made—but shades of my cremated assassin and his ashes! The two thoughts are born of the same mother; indeed, they are twin brothers.

Sir James Frazer sums up the present position of the civilized and uncivilized worlds by averring that "a survey of the existing races of mankind shows them to be distinguished from one another by a variety of religions, but that these distinctions are not merely coterminous with the broad distinctions of race, but honeycomb the town, the village, and even the family, so that the surface of society all over the world is cracked and scarred with rents and fissures opened up by the disintegrating influence of religious dissension. Yet when we have penetrated through these differences which affect mainly the intelligent part of the community, we shall find a solid stratum of intellectual agreement among the dull, the ignorant, and the superstitious, who constitute unfortunately the vast majority of mankind. It is not very far beneath our feet in Europe at the present day, and it crops up in the heart of the Australian wilderness. This universal faith, this catholic creed, is a belief in the efficacy of magic. While religious systems differ even in the same country in different eyes, the system of sympathetic magic remains everywhere and at all times substantially alike in its principles and practice. Among the ignorant and superstitious classes of modern Europe it is very much what it was thousands of years ago in Egypt and India, and what it now is among the lowest savages surviving in the remotest corners of the world".

If, then, we may accept Sir James's contention (and I personally think we can), it means that mankind is now divided into two groups, the one, and the far larger, still groping in the primeval forest of magic, where in some cases a few rays of light have penetrated; the other and smaller beginning to emerge from the jungle twilight and to see the light of day beyond, but still with many undergrowths to cut away and burn before it becomes entirely free from superstition and magic. So that, if we set out to compare two countries in this regard, wherever they may be situated, the difference is merely one of degree, and not of kind.

This emergence of mankind from the primeval forest represents evolution in its true sense, and all the various religious systems expounded in the last three thousand years have been but a necessary corollary to that emergence, since man, once he loses his belief in magic, must look round for some other and higher reason to account for the Universe and its governance.

To come now to Siam and our own stories in particular, the burying of figures is only one of many similar practices still in vogue in this country, which are concerned with the active principles of love. There was the recent case of a domestic servant in the house of one of my Siamese friends who was being pestered by the attentions of a young soldier, which, however, roused no answering flutterings in the girl's heart. What did he do? He obtained by stealth a small phial of oil, oil extracted from a human corpse, and seeking a suitable opportunity, he uncorked the phial and flung the contents over the unsuspecting girl. In a practice of this kind there are said to be two alternative results. Either the lady will be fired with a deep and lasting passion for the thrower, or she will go mad. In this case the young lady chose the latter course.

Another practice, of which I cannot point to any specific instance, but which is said to be not uncommon, is concerned with the recapture of erring husbands, who have strayed from their family *mensa et thoro*.

There is a heavily built boat called a 'sampan', in common use on the main river of Siam for the conveyance of passengers, which is propelled by one man with a single oar standing in the stern. All that the injured wife has to do is to collect a little of the water from under the boards at the bottom of *seven* sampans, mix it in a bottle, and give it to her husband to drink, of course unbeknown to him. It is said to be an excellent corrective, but cases have been known where the result was different from that desired. In fact, in spite of the mystic number seven, this practice must, it would appear, be fraught with hazard at all times.

These practices (of which the record may expose me to suspicion and calumny) will seem to us, even if believed, childish in the extreme, and yet at the bottom they differ scarcely at all from the examples of sympathetic magic given above, as having recently happened in England.

Some educated people are almost entirely free from superstitions, possibly more by chance than by any superiority of intelligence. It seems to be a question of one's turn or bent of mind. If you are entirely occupied with the charms of the girl opposite you at dinner, or if your mind is of an epicurean turn, and becomes quickly immersed in the menu and the wine list, or if you are calculating whether to go on holding those tin shares or not, the probability is that you won't notice whether you are sitting thirteen at table or not. But there is no doubt that many otherwise educated people will not sit thirteen at table, will still persist in throwing spilt salt over their left shoulder, and will not get married in the month of May, and do not consider their superstitions in any way childish, which, in fact, they are, just like the more sensational ones already quoted. It is only a question of degree, though I admit there is a wide difference between the two in the result of their practice. Still, these trivial and uneventful superstitions must be a relic of the not very distant past, when education had not yet begun its work of differentiation among the peoples of the world. They are enough to prove what is only too often forgotten, namely, that all the peoples of this earth are fundamentally one.

II

I DO not know why, but the subject of ghouls has a relish for me that few other subjects possess. I like to sit and think and gloat over them, metaphorically but lovingly rolling them in my hands as I would a fine piece of early Chinese porcelain. That story of Amina in the *Arabian Nights* has remained with me ever since my boyhood, and I never think of her without a sense of intense 'ghoulish' delight. I do not know that I myself possess any ghoulish properties—I understand from those who are qualified to judge that I do not—but somewhere within me is a chord which rings and responds to the mere mention of their name.

A Siamese friend deprecates this feeling of mine very seriously, and quotes me an old saying, by which I think he means to convey the sense of our own proverb, "Where ignorance is bliss, 'tis folly to be wise". But I cannot prevent this feeling, and I have been at some pains to inquire into the nature of ghouls, so that I may recognize them if I see them.

If I remember rightly, Amina used to climb over the cemetery wall, dig up the dead bodies and eat them. Siamese ghouls do not eat dead bodies—*they pluck the livers out of living bodies*; and in *An Asian Arcady* I gave an instance of my own personal experience at Lampang of my pony-boy, who was compelled to leave the city with his whole family because his mother had been convicted by the elders of the commune of being a ghoul. Ghouls are of both sexes, both male and female, and the special feature which characterizes them is that they have no pupils to their eyes, and therefore cannot look other people in the face. Needless to say, they can see just the same; indeed, they must be able to see much better than most people, since they can locate the exact spot in the body where the liver resides, and pluck it out cleanly, without visible contact.

The quality of ghoulishness is said to be hereditary and to pass from mother to daughter, or from father to son, by some form of physical contact, the secret of which is guarded very closely. Naturally it is not easy to detect a ghoul, and convictions are usually pronounced on suspicion, for ghouls do not go out by day, but only at night, and then they leave their concrete bodies behind, calmly sleeping on the floor, while their astral bodies play hide-and-seek with their victims in the shape of the *ignis fatuus*, or will-o'-the-wisp. With all the stagnant water lying around the villages, especially in the country districts during the rains, miasma is continually rising, and at night the *ignis fatuus* must be a common sight all over Siam. The peasant mind must account for this unearthly light somehow or other, and so the belief gradually arises that here is the dreaded ghoul on the look-out for the unwary. It is not at all uncommon for folk to sit up at night to try and prevent a ghoul from entering their house.

The *ignis fatuus* can, however, play another rôle in the people's minds. Some years ago, on the banks of the river Me Nān at Pitsanulok, a stationary light was to be seen every night without any apparent reason to account for it, and such became its fame that people flocked to see it from all over Siam, from as far south as Petchaburi, in the fond hope that they had at last discovered the elixir of life. Eventually this pilgrimage became rather a nuisance to the Government, and an official chemist, who was sent up to investigate, promptly discovered that the cause of the light was a mass of decaying vegetation buried just beneath the soil. Thus was one more fond illusion shattered. But this is by the way.

When the ghoul has selected its victim, it usually plans to attack him in the closet if he can catch him there, so that when an attack is expected, the householder will strew thorns all over the floor, and thus will effectually keep it out. Before they go to bed the women of the house, having bathed, will hang out their 'panung' and 'pahom' and other clothes to dry overnight, and if in the morning they find on any part of them a peculiar, clearly marked ring, they always know that a ghoul has been hovering round and has wiped its mouth on the cloth.

The whole question of 'phi' or spirits is a fascinating subject, and to deal with it faithfully and exhaustively would require a book in itself. But I heard of a case the other day, which I think worth recording, of a person being unintentionally attacked by a spirit and thereby becoming dangerously ill.

It seems that the spirit-doctors are in the habit of 'keeping' a number of spirits in their houses, which they do by acquiring a number of human skulls in which the spirits reside. Every seven days they have to let some of these spirits loose, or they may be liable to attacks themselves. By chance it happened on one occasion, when such a spirit was let loose, that a young girl was in its way. It immediately and unthinkingly attacked her, dived deep into her body and consumed her, bringing about a state of acute consumption. The witch-doctor, who was sent for at once, said he was able to perform a cure by drawing out of her body quantities of thorns, pieces of wood, and all kinds of impurities.

To effect this cure his remedy was as follows: He took flour, mixed it with water, and then, with the necessary incantations, spread it over the flesh. When he removed it in due course, he took away the impurities with it.

In the case in question, unfortunately, the remedy did not work, for the girl died within three months. The evil power was too strong.

I have in several of the stories referred to the symbolic use of water, and in these instances the meaning is reasonably clear that it represents a kind of purification. But recently a Siamese related to me an interesting ceremony called "Truat Nam", or "The Water Examination", at which he presided some years ago, and which is not so obvious in its meaning.

He had bought a small property near a village on the southern coast, and it happened that, when he came to take possession, the village was being agitated by a violent quarrel which had arisen between one of the principal villagers and another young man resident there, but of no particular standing. The reason for the quarrel may, perhaps, be guessed.

The gentleman of substance, who owned a large fishing-smack as well as buffaloes and a cart or two, had in his capacity of fisherman-farmer reached the dignity of a three-wife man. But whether he did not pay sufficient attention to the charms of the third lady, or whether she did not appreciate his addresses, or disliked playing third string to his bow, the upshot was that she began to set her cap at another young villager, more to her taste and liking, even as in our tale of "The Snare", who conceived it to be his duty to comfort disconsolate ladies; and many were the visits of consolation which he paid to her in the course of his duty. At length the husband discovered how he was being deceived, and in his jealous heart he determined to lie in wait for the young gallant, and teach him that bow-strings were private property. So he hid himself in his garden, and one dark night, surprising the young man as he was climbing over the fence, ran at him with a cry, and plunged his keen-pointed dagger between the wretch's shoulder blades. The young lover wrenched himself free and took refuge behind a large tree, and such was the blind fury of the husband that in his second rush he missed his aim entirely, and drove his dagger deep into the tree-trunk—so deep that he could not withdraw it, and the man escaped with a severe but not mortal wound. When he recovered, the lover was all for pursuing the husband at law for a wanton and serious bodily attack, and it was at this stage of the play that my friend arrived. All the village was mightily agog with the *crime passionnel* that had taken place, and fears were expressed on all sides that one of the men would surely kill the other. Eventually the elders of the village waited on my friend, and asked him to mediate between the two, and try to compose their quarrel, assuring him that they would be responsible for bringing the young gallant to a proper and reasonable frame of mind. So my friend sent for the husband, and although at first he avowed that he could not set eyes on the young man without a violent desire to kill him, yet in the end he was persuaded to agree, not only to forgive him freely, but even to give up the third wife, so that she might marry the man on whom she was set.

But this pardon had to take place in public, if it was to be effective, and accordingly the stage was set for the ceremony in my friend's house. The first to arrive was the husband, accompanied by a large number of villagers, and when they had taken their seats on the floor, the offender was brought in, bearing in his hand a lighted candle, which he offered to the husband in token of worship and purification. Then he went down on his knees and bowed his head three times to the floor. At this, the husband solemnly gave his word that he pardoned him, and would not molest him in any way in the future, and furthermore that he would give up the lady to him to be his wife. Having repeated the necessary formula before the assembled folk, the husband took a vessel full of water, and having poured the water from this vessel into another, emptied it slowly, drop by drop, on to the ground below. The ceremony was then at an end.

The symbolism in this use of water is not here, as it might be with us, a sign of purification, of ridding oneself of sin such as anger or evil thoughts, or even of denying all further responsibility, as in the case of Pontius Pilate and the phraseology we have formed from that scene. The idea behind the ceremony is that Mother Earth will receive and preserve your merit, and reward you and yours in due time. It is done, in witness of making merit, as a sign that one wishes to share this merit with everybody of whom one is thinking at the time. In performing such an act we should deliberately associate it with people we know or have known, whether alive or dead, whether in heaven or hell, and pray that they may receive a share of whatever merit we earn from the act we perform. Even the animal creatures of the world may be included in the dedication.

Thus, through the instrumentality of my friend, the drama ended happily instead of in tragedy, and the parties are said to be living in the same village still on excellent terms. The wrong done has been purged by forgiveness, and the peace kept by oaths not lightly to be broken. But the husband was very greedy to want *three* wives!

III

IN thinking of his mother's slave in the story of Nai Prasop you must not conjure up a picture of batches of slaves impressed to work in plantations like the negroes of Africa were in America and the West Indies a century or two ago. In his *History of Siam* Wood says that slavery was unknown in the days of Ram Kamheng, the first Thai king, and his successors at Sukhothai in the thirteenth century, but was a feature of the social system during the whole period of the Ayudhya dynasty from 1350 to 1767. It was apparently always a form of debt slavery, and lasted in one form or another down to modern times; indeed, until the year 1905, when King Chulalongkorn finally abolished it. No doubt the masters were able, in the main, to use their slaves as they pleased in the old days, and were acknowledged, indeed, as lord of life over them; but that the slaves were not entirely ignored is shown by the fact that in 1637 a law of slavery was passed, containing, among others, provisions for the punishment of masters who killed or injured their slaves, and also setting forth various means by which slaves could regain their liberty. The chief method, as a rule, as the story relates, was by being bought out or redeemed by somebody else; but sometimes, if the slaves found a good master, they were very content to remain in the household, as they gained considerable advantages by doing so, such as protection and free food in return for their services. Knowing the Siamese passably well, I have little doubt that a great many of the slaves became such by selling and attaching themselves and their families to the households of important men. Although they were prisoners in a sense, yet they probably did not have a superabundance of work to do, and it gave them a kind of prestige to be called so-and-so's man. The punishment meted out to the disobedient, and to the offender in word or deed, was certain to be severe and swift, but it is not necessary to draw the inevitable conclusion that the slave's lot was altogether a miserable one in Siam in the past centuries. By saying this I do not wish to seem to condone the system, but to draw in true perspective the outline of one which was the outcome of the times and of the conditions of life prevailing.

There is still a practice in vogue of selling one's services for a lump sum, and then working it off at four ticals a month. The master pays for food and clothing, sometimes educates the children of the family, and, as a rule, will allow the debt to be redeemed at rather more than four ticals a month. All this system actually amounts to now is an advance of wages on entering service, and here the master runs a considerable risk unless he knows the servant's family personally. A friend of mine not so long ago was kind, or foolish, enough to advance the sum of eighty ticals to a newly hired woman-servant, but she disappeared the following day, and has not been seen since.

The so-called black art of astrology has been for many centuries in vogue in Siam, and is still a good deal practised to-day. In the country villages it does not, I am afraid, rest upon any scientific basis, and the 'maw doo', or astrologer, has probably to live more by his wits than by any precise knowledge of the art. It is very common to see a countryman tattooed on the chest or back with his horoscope, but I am told that this can seldom be taken as accurately cast, and that it is used purely and simply as a charm to render the wearer invulnerable to bullets and knives.

In Bangkok, however, the subject is of considerable

interest to a number of students, but it is generally recognized that there is great difficulty in casting, as the exact minute of birth must be known if the horoscope is to be accurately cast. The method of casting is said to be practically the same as in Europe, and a short time ago I heard of a case which is worth recording. An aviator went up on a survey trip, became lost, and was not heard of for a week. His wife was naturally greatly alarmed, and in her anxiety went to consult a well educated student of astrology. He cast her husband's horoscope, and told her that she need not feel anxious, as her husband was alive, and she would have news of him in two days' time. Sure enough it turned out as he had said, and it appeared that the aviator had lost his way in a fog, and had come down somewhere near the Burmese border, far away from any town or habitation, and it took several days for the party to get into touch with the authorities. Of course, this may have been pure coincidence, just good guesswork, and I would not recommend the study to any but the most sceptical, as I heard of another case where a young Siamese judge became so infatuated with the study of astrology that he eventually became insane and had to be shut up.

Astrology and alchemy are supposed to go hand in hand, and the story of "The Missing Element" is not, even in these days, so imaginative as many conceive it to be. The art of mixing metals has always made a great appeal to the Siamese, especially for the fashioning of images of the Buddha, of which a countless number have been cast during the last thousand years. The most prized of all are those made of a composition called 'Samrit', which consists of a mixture of three, five, or seven metals according to the prescription. The result is a dark olive-brown colour, which takes on a beautiful patina with age, and the price of a good 'Samrit' image is at least double that of an ordinary bronze Buddha. There is also another composition called 'Nāk', which is chiefly copper, but which contains a good percentage of gold, up to, some say, as much as 20 per cent. Images made of this composition have a deep rich copper-red colour, and seldom require much polishing to keep them bright.

It is this ingrained love of mixing metals which has turned their thoughts to alchemy, and to attempts to transmute the baser metals into gold and silver. The last case of which I heard happened only a few years ago. An elderly Siamese market-gardener, living on the west bank of the river Menam in Bukkalo, a suburb of Bangkok, became smitten with the game, and hired a 'kru', or teacher, to expound to him the mysteries of changing copper into silver. The experiments lasted a number of years, during which time the old man spent most of his substance in the sure belief that he would be eventually rewarded with all the riches of the world; but when at length the appointed day arrived for the first delivery of silver, the 'kru' was nowhere to be found, and has not appeared since. In a very short time the poor old man, bowed down with misery and poverty, died in a condition bordering on insanity.

IV

A RICE-GROWING village in Siam stands out among the padi fields, especially during the dry season, like an oasis in the desert. It appears from a distance to be a mass of trees surrounded by a fence, but in reality the compounds are contiguous, and each compound builds its own bamboo fence to define its area and as a measure of self-protection. The entrance to the village is by a narrow lane which winds in all directions in and out among the compounds. Indeed, once you are in a village, you seem to be in a kind of maze. A village of this nature will consist of anything from twenty to fifty houses, and is usually without a market-place. There are, of course, larger villages of a hundred houses and more, each with its own market-place, but such villages will usually be found on the banks of rivers and canals, or nowadays near the railway-line. In the larger villages the people are, alas, fast becoming sophisticated, and in these a school will usually be found in the temple grounds, where the children are taught to read and write, whose fathers and mothers could not.

But the picture I wish to draw is one of the small villages in the heart of the padi fields, where life is still largely communal, and "arcadian simplicity vies with rustic kindliness". The house is usually in the middle of the compound, which is enclosed by a fence of stout bamboo. It is raised above the ground, and rests on piles or posts made of some hard wood as a protection against water, thieves, and animals. There is a narrow path up to the steps, which are often detachable and can be pulled up when the family retire at night. There is an outside verandah running the length of the house, and two or three rooms inside slightly raised above the verandah, the number of rooms varying according to the size of the family or the dignity of the owner. The framework of the house is made of bamboo, with hard wood posts for the tie-beams, and the roof is made of attap, which is the dried leaf of the Nipa palm.

Each village has a 'Pū Yai Bān', or village headman, for every ten houses, and these form the village council to settle its affairs as far as possible. A number of villages all close together will be under the charge of a 'Kamnan'. The duties of the 'Pū Yai Bān' are to instruct the people how to pay their taxes, and generally to act *in loco parentis* to the families under his care. If they are lazy in their field duty, a good 'Pū Yai Bān' will stir them to work, and one particular duty may be mentioned of beating a gong at the cry of thief to summon all the villagers to help to catch him. In such villages as these there is no temple, and this will usually be found in some isolated spot some distance away. In the old days a secluded and far-away spot was always chosen for the site of a temple, so that the priests might be able to meditate in peace and quiet. In the course of time a number of villages would spring up at a distance all around it. This distance may vary from a quarter of a mile to over a mile in cases where the country-side is sparsely populated, but it must not be too far from the village for the priests to make their daily visits to receive their food. This is the first act of the day. As soon as the people have risen and cooked their food, the priests arrive with their begging-bowls. The priests must rise at four o'clock. A gong is rung, which is the signal for the priests to don the yellow robe and say their prayers. Then they set out very early and reach the village between six and seven. If you are an early riser, you can see them wending their way slowly and separately over the fields toward the village. They will visit the houses in turn, and are not allowed to refuse any of the food offered; but once their bowls are full, the villagers will offer no more. They then return to their temple, in single file, as they came. Buddhist etiquette demands that the priest should not speak or show any sign of emotion. He gives no thanks. Indeed, the giving of food to the priests confers a blessing on the giver, and the thanks are rather due to the priest for coming. The food given is always rice with either eggs, or fish, or meat (as a luxury), curry, and a vegetable salad. Only rice and eggs and such objects will be put in the bowl. Curries or salads will be put in dishes and carried separately. If more than one priest come to the same village, they approach and enter in single file and none will speak to the other. They come, receive their food, and go in silence. When one priest has gone, another may come to the same house, and if the family has a plentiful supply, they will fill his bowl too; if they have not, they will merely retire, and the priest, as a rule, will realise that he must go elsewhere. The giver, who is usually the head of the family, will show respect by sitting on the ground in the Siamese fashion and offer the food to the priest standing before him, who will then bend to receive it. The priests make only one collection, but take two meals daily, one at eight o'clock and the other at eleven o'clock in the morning. When once they have gone, the family have their own meal, consisting of the same fare as they have given to the priest. It is a strict custom that they must not eat out of the main pot or dish until they have given their food to the priests. They sit round in a circle, with a large flat tray in the middle, containing the different foods to be eaten, each in a separate dish. The rice is brought to the meal in the main pot from the kitchen, and each one of the family takes his share of rice with a large spoon which goes the round. Each dish has also its own spoon, in the old days made of brass, but now usually of porcelain, with which the eater helps himself. He will then mix the curry with the rice in his bowl and eat it with his fingers. Very often the family take their meal in the kitchen; if not, then usually on the verandah. Water is sometimes taken direct as needed from large porous jars on the verandah, and at others is put in small brass bowls beside each member of the family. If fruits or cakes are at hand, then they are eaten after the rice and curry. This custom of eating with the fingers must have come from India, and not from China, where chopsticks are always used. As a rule, the peasants take three meals a day—in the early morning, at noon, and at four o'clock in the afternoon. After eating, the tray of betel-nut with its accessories and the spittoon appear, indispensable articles in every household.

When they have had their early and noontide meals, they go out to work. In the planting season the men plough and the women sow, or if the rice is to be transplanted, then both sexes will work. The children will be used for looking after the cattle and for scaring the birds away while the rice is growing. Later in the season you will see in the middle of the fields a little watchtower rearing its head high above the padi. This is erected for men to watch the whole night through as harvest time approaches, to prevent thieves from reaping the padi while the owners sleep.

When the family go to bed, they sleep on rush mats, with an oblong pillow stuffed with kapok until it is very hard. The whole family sleep together in the same room, until the children reach a certain age, when they sleep apart. Under the house the buffaloes, cattle, and horses are kept, and if the women weave cloth in the dry season, you will find their looms under the house as well; but in Central Siam not very much weaving is done nowadays, and the cloth is nearly all imported. In the compound there is a granary for storing padi, a huge round bamboo tub with a roof-shed over it. There will be banana-trees, and sometimes fruit-trees, such as mango or jack-fruit, in the compound, shading the house, and one or two pariah dogs will be always at hand.

There you have a Siamese peasant family at home.

There is nothing, therefore, inherently improbable in four wandering priests putting up at a deserted temple near a village, as described in "The Four Jolly Robbers". Commonly, such wandering priests sleep in large white umbrella-tents which they carry with them and stick in the ground, in a field, or on the bank of a river, or anywhere else convenient. But if they should find a deserted temple, they might equally well camp in that. There is a difference, though, between wandering and resident priests. First, they are often thought to be more holy and righteous than the local priests, on the analogy of the old proverb that "no prophet is without honour save in his own country". Secondly, they do not go round begging their food from the villagers. On the contrary, if they give it out that they are going to stay, the villagers will come to them, as they did to the venerable old priest in "The Buried Figures". Wandering priests never carry food with them, and if the peasants bring them food, well and good; if they do not, they must go without and strive to emulate that band of pilgrims who set out to catch the weasel asleep.

> For those who sail the scented seas,
> Don't hunger or grow thin;
> They feast upon the scenery,
> And drink its beauties in.

I have known those airy, jaunty lines for thirty years and more, but I cannot recall who wrote them.

Their object is to seek quiet and meditation or to do penance, and thereby to make merit; but it is also to preach the doctrine, the Buddha, the Law, and the Order, the Holy Triple Gems. They are to be found all over Siam, and usually travel in twos and threes at a time; but if they carry their own tents with them, they must pitch them far apart at night, so as to be free to pray and fast, safe from the temptation to talk and allow their minds to dwell on worldly things. Most of such wandering priests have remained in the priesthood for many years before they start to travel.

In the story of "The Four Jolly Robbers", the saying, "Going to the Bodhi tree for their initiation into the Order," is a euphemistic expression for saying that the four rascals were false priests. It arises from the fact that in some cases rogues do literally go to the sacred Bodhi (Bō) tree, which represents the Buddha, before they falsely don the yellow robe, hoping thereby to ease their minds and consciences, and possibly to escape the punishment for their present sins in the next life.

In the same story reference is made to domestic animals being set free in the temple grounds. It is a common custom for the people to do so, for the temple grounds are a place of refuge and considered holy ground. Thereby the giver obtains merit and the animals remain until they die, unless they are killed or removed by mischievous people. But such an act would be a great sin.

Both the temples and the priests are held in great veneration all over the country.

Temple land is sacred wherever it lies, and by a very ancient law it is laid down that "once temple land, always temple land". The people themselves would never dream of erecting a house or a building on or even next to a temple site, however ruined and deserted, and it is a superstition strongly held that anyone who did so would inevitably meet with disaster. There are said to be many notable instances of this. I have, however, reasons for thinking that in respect of very ancient temples this rule is becoming somewhat relaxed.

As for the priests, mothers always try and persuade their sons to enter the priesthood if only for a short time. The Buddhist priesthood is not like the Christian, an ordination for life, and a priest can always retire into secular life again at will. But by entering the priesthood the man brings not only merit to himself, but vicariously to his parents as well, especially to the mother who bore him, as in "The Story of Nai Prasop".

On the other hand, nuns are not held in such respect or considered on the same plane as priests. A daughter can become a nun, but she is in fact little better than a lay-woman, and the rules of conduct are not very strict, as they are for priests. For example, a nun might make a loud noise in eating, without offence, but for a priest to do so would be a grave breach of etiquette. He must eat quietly and not open his mouth. Also, he must not get up noisily or suddenly from his seat, but quietly and gently move away.

This deportment on the part of priests is looked upon with great admiration by the lay people, and probably the most subtle compliment ever paid to the English by a Siamese was uttered by an old Court official of King Chulalongkorn's reign. This official, in the course of his duties, came frequently in contact with both priests and English officials and guests, and he was so struck with the quietness and unobtrusiveness of the demeanour of the latter, that he remarked to his son, "Englishmen are like Buddhist priests", than which, in his view, he could pay them no higher compliment. It speaks well for the Englishmen who came to Siam in the Fifth Reign.

V

THE Siamese have the reputation of being a singularly modest people, that is, modest in their person, and, as far as I am able to judge, the reputation is well deserved. But this modesty of person, which is carried to such a length that neither sex will strip entirely naked when bathing alone, does not entail any secrecy about the biological facts of life.

It is not usual for parents to talk about these matters before their children, nor for children to ask direct questions, nor for brothers and sisters to discuss them together; but both boys and girls can learn them gradually from the general family life of the house, because there is no attempt to hide them. For instance, a mother, if angry with her child, will say to it: "What's the use of bearing you?" Or she may tease it by saying: "You are not my child; Father found you floating on the river in a basket"; and the child, who knows already, will answer: 'No, I came out of your stomach," at the same time pointing to it with its finger. Also, when a mother bears a second and subsequent children, the elder child will notice this, and may sometimes be heard boasting to his school-fellows that his mother has given birth to another child.

Yet a girl, however indirectly she might come to learn the facts of life, would never be told by her mother what would be expected of her on marriage. She would be left to find out herself, and in this respect the Siamese resemble our own race.

The gaining of sexual knowledge among children of the humblest classes is also helped by the kind of repartee common among their elders. If a man and a woman, not his wife, quarrel violently, as sometimes happens, the man will clinch the argument by accusing the woman of having had intercourse with himself, which is the greatest insult that he can offer; and she will retort in the same vein. It is a common form of vituperation, and children naturally hear this, and soon come to realize its meaning. The same might be said, I suppose, with a good deal of truth of our own lowest classes; not much is left to the children's imagination.

As regards modesty of person, although adults never bathe naked even in the privacy of their own rooms, children, both boys and girls, even up to the age of thirteen or fourteen, used to be seen bathing naked in the canals. This is not such a common sight as it was, and nowadays, although, perhaps, boys at school will bathe together naked, girls over the age of eight or nine will scarcely ever be seen doing so. It would still be thought a shameless thing for an older girl to bathe naked in her own room. Even to doctors the Siamese are very loth to show their bodies, and will only do so if necessity compels. It used to be said that a woman did not mind exposing her breasts after she had become a mother, but it is rare to see such a sight now in any class, and practically all women wear the 'pahom' round the upper part of their bodies. I once heard, while travelling, that in some district or other in the vicinity of the Mekhong there was a tribe living of which the women went about naked from the waist downwards; and the reason they gave was that everybody had seen the lower part of their bodies from their childhood days, but that their breasts they had grown themselves, and they were not, therefore, for the public gaze! Plausible, but I suspect a traveller's tale.

This treatment of the bodily functions is all part of Siamese 'realism', which is no doubt the outcome of their religious teaching. In this way they are a very natural people, and among the members of a family no suggestion of prurience will arise regarding these matters. Some people will no doubt hold that such an attitude of mind could only be found in a fairly primitive state of society, but yet I think it would be an 'advance' on our part if parents were to educate and guide, by natural answers to natural questions, our own children in the matter of bodily functions and the biological processes of life. It can be done, if the parents are sufficiently educated themselves, in a simple, reverent, and truthful way, and it would save a deal of tragedy and mental agony in store for some of our children when they grow to man's and especially woman's estate. It is by making a mystery of our organic functions that the mischief is caused.

Children in Siam come to the age of puberty at the age of about fourteen for boys and twelve for girls. Nowadays children are becoming more precocious, and it is not altogether uncommon for a girl in Bangkok to take a husband at the age of fourteen. But it was a rare occurrence fifty years ago, and a girl who did so would have been the talk of the village. In those days a girl would sometimes stay at home and remain unmarried until she was twenty-five or even thirty. She would help her parents in looking after the house and the other children, and when she did get married she would still be considered a young bride. If a suitor sent to ask for her hand at an earlier age, her parents would put him off by saying that she was too young and knew nothing of life and its responsibilities, meaning thereby that she was not yet trained enough in her duties to become a good housewife.

It should not be rashly concluded that, because polygamy is permitted in Siam, it was or is the normal order of the day. As I have stated in *An Asian Arcady*, economic conditions play a great part in deciding this question, and in Siam I would hazard a guess that

90 per cent. of its inhabitants were and are habitually monogamous, for one reason only, if for no other, that the numbers of men and women are almost identical. At least the preponderance of women is much smaller than in most other countries. It is only the comparatively wealthy who can afford the luxury of a number of wives.

The usual marriage customs have been so often described, by others as well as myself, that I will not go over the ground again. But it may be emphasized that even to-day in some parts of the country the parties concerned do not speak to one another, and only know of one another by hearsay, until a day is appointed for the parties to meet to see if the marriage is to be arranged or not. Then, if either finds the other distasteful, it is no disgrace to declare the marriage 'off', though such drastic action would naturally be only resorted to on extreme occasions. Also the parents of the man always employ an intermediary with those of the girl, as it would be considered an insult if they went themselves. There are no child, or infant, marriages or betrothals in Siam, as in China or India; but among the young people of the humble classes elopement is common, and then the girl will naturally come to live at the house of the man's parents. Later in such cases the man will send intermediaries with gifts to ask for pardon, which is usually granted. As a race the Siamese are of a forgiving nature, which is largely due to the Buddhist teaching to return good, and not evil, for evil. It is firmly believed that, if evil is returned, its effect will go on indefinitely through countless lives and impede one's ascent towards Nirvana. Nor, as a rule, are they easily irritated, and it is a rare sight to see a Siamese excited, unless he is under the influence of liquor. They are, if anything, rather too passive and easy-going, a result which is no doubt due to the easy conditions of living.

In most classes of Siam the standard of sexual morality still remains reasonably high. Girls rarely go about unchaperoned, and it would be considered almost immoral for a man to touch a young girl. One mental attitude may be recorded, which to us will seem singular. Hand-shaking between the two sexes of the upper classes is now no longer taboo, but it is not so long ago that for a man to clasp a girl by the hand could only mean one thing—that he desired her.

Looking at the subject of morality from another angle, the Siamese do not care to look upon nude statues or nude pictures. If such were to be seen in a house, folk of the old school would condemn them as bringing an evil influence into the house, and they would probably look upon their owner as a lustful man. This attitude is probably due, as with us, to old-fashioned ideas, as well as to a failure to appreciate, indeed, to a complete ignorance of classical art in any form.

In literature sexual matters are nearly always treated as a matter for joking, and are not intended to convey any suggestive or salacious meaning. At least, this is not the first motive behind the story. Even girls will read aloud passages from broad stories without attempting to read into them anything of a pornographic nature. It is one of the Siamese forms of humour, just as it was in early days in Europe, and this brings us to a consideration of Siamese humour in general.

VI

IF I were to ask you, dear reader, an honest question, would you, on your part, give me an honest answer? I will take you on trust and risk it—which of these fifteen stories have you enjoyed reading most, and, if you have read any of them more than once, which are they? Should I be hazarding a stupid guess if I suggested, "The Effect of Truth", or "The Snare", or "The Love Lesson"? I wonder!

Yet I for my part have honestly not included these three wicked stories merely in order to corrupt your morals, but rather to show you the type of humour which the Siamese appreciate and enjoy. After all, as my Editor avers, it all depends upon how the stories are told. And he has been so delicate himself in his treatment of them that I have not found it at all necessary to improve upon him.

But an Italian friend of mine, who has read them in English, has tried to take the wind out of my sails by telling me that the stories are not Siamese at all, but directly borrowed from Boccaccio and other mediæval writers. I was about to take this as rather a compliment to my literary powers, but any such feeling was promptly quashed by his adding that, of course, he was not referring to the style of Boccaccio, which was so delicate as to be inimitable, but only to the characterization and flavour of the stories.

I admit that appearances are in favour of his contention, and, as I have myself remarked in the preface, they bring Chaucer (in our own country) to our minds at once; but, as we all know, appearances are sometimes deceitful, and when we consider the circumstances and the nature of the people, I do not think there are any substantial grounds for this supposition. In the first place, the Siamese people, up to the last fifty or sixty years, have had very little contact with the West (except for a period in the sixteenth and seventeenth centuries), and, as far as direct literary borrowings go, have only within very recent years begun to borrow from the West. It is scarcely conceivable that the Portuguese brought Boccaccio and the others with them in the sixteenth century and translated them into Siamese. Secondly, the Siamese themselves have a fund of proverbs which deal with the relations between the sexes, and which are obviously the result of their own cogitation. "An old slave or a loving wife, put not your trust in these"; "Three days' absence from your wife and her heart is another's"; "Man is padi, woman is rice". These proverbs are not borrowed from anywhere, least of all from the West, and almost proclaim their indigenous origin. So that if we couple the improbability of borrowing from the West with the undoubted authenticity of their proverbs, we can scarcely help but conclude that the stories themselves present a true picture of Siamese thought and humour. For a more probable answer to the riddle, we come, then, back to what I have already said: that, as regards many facets, and the deeper cut ones, of their life, the bulk of the Siamese people are now in the same stage of evolution as Europe was in the Middle Ages, during the time of the Feudal System.

"The Effect of Truth" is pure Chaucer, and is exactly what one would expect of a people in a Chaucerian age. It is broad, but it is straightforward, and it is true to life. There is nothing suggestive, nothing pornographic whatever about the story, and if you have been freely among the peasants, you can see those three people sitting round the bowl of water just as clearly as you can see your own family sitting round a breakfast-table.

The sudden call; the husband's anxiety, and finally despair; the remembrance that he had fed the priest for three days running; the priest's realization of the futility of charms; the sheepishness of the man and his wife on being challenged in their most vulnerable spot; and the wife's woman-like anger at her husband's faithlessness. Why, almost the whole gamut of human sensations are contained in that one short story—pleasure, pride, fear, anxiety, despair, hope, faith, weakness, strength, anger, jealousy, shyness, hate—all are there, well and evenly mixed in the brewing. Can you tell me a more human story, or picture a more human scene? In reading it, one need not jump to the conclusion that this incident could happen in every Siamese family, and that it is typical of all Siamese life, but it might undoubtedly apply to any peasant family.

The two stories, named "The Snare" and "The Love Lesson", partake more of the nature of the Decameron than of Chaucer, *without, of course, Boccaccio's immortal style*, and are excellent examples of stories which would be generally read and enjoyed. The ladies would perhaps feel a little embarrassment, and would certainly resent the attacks on their sex which the stories contain. Yet even they would enjoy the humour of them, and especially the clever way in which the husbands are made to look foolish. It is, no doubt, highly regrettable that the men should have such a low opinion of their women-folk as to make such terrible proverbs and write such immoral stories about them; but still it must be remarked that the laugh always rests with the lady against the husband, who is pictured as a dolt, and easily gulled. The conversation between the old man and his son in "The Snare" is as happy a conceit as imagination could contrive. The scene and the argument are both as clear as a polished mirror. In "The Love Lesson" one of the nicest of touches is when the wife manages to incriminate the husband by going to feed the baby, and then deprives him of all defence or excuse by her attack in the morning. The tales are told in the original Siamese without giving any semblance of offence by the use of coarse or obscene language, and it is clear that, without minimizing in any way the value of the sex interest to the tale, it is the subtleties and manœuvres by which the wife outwits the husband that give the chief delight to the Siamese mind rather than the salacious side of the story.

The Siamese, indeed, have as a race a very keen sense of humour, which is by no means confined to sexual affairs, or requires a direct sexual flavour to make them of interest. As an example of another kind of humour let me whisper the following tale.

There is a kind of anagram used by the Siamese to denote the people of certain provinces, which takes the form of 'Ko-ka-la-su'. You will appreciate why I have used the word 'whisper' when I say that I dare not indicate more precisely the names of the four provinces to which the anagram refers, since the esoteric meaning of it is that their inhabitants are not as reliable as they might be in the matter of veracity or general trustworthiness. They have an unenviable reputation for saying one thing and meaning another. The reproach is, I believe, one of some antiquity, and nowadays the people involved will become highly indignant and very warm at the use of it, saying that they are as honest and upright Siamese as those from any other province. So it has to be spoken with bated breath, and I am almost 'braving the elements' in going as far as I have. Wild horses would not drag the actual names of the provinces out of me.

Well, the story goes that in the principal city of one of these provinces there was a certain open hall, where the chief wits and wags used to foregather of an evening to exercise their fertile minds, which went by the name of "Sālā Gōhok", or "The Hall of Lies". One day a Siamese visitor from Bangkok came to this city, and, meeting with a party of wags, asked them if they would show him the famous "Hall of Lies", of which he had heard so often. Like a flash and without any hesitation one of them replied: "I am sorry, but I cannot; it has just been removed to Bangkok", which gave great satisfaction to the party as being a gem of repartee. If you can visualize mentally the full implications of both the question and the answer, then you will have obtained an excellent impression of one kind of Siamese humour.

An example of another kind—and a very representative one—will be found in the lecture given before the Siam Society some years ago by a Siamese member on "The Pastime of Rhyme-making and Singing in Rural Siam". The lecture, which was afterwards printed in the Journal of the Siam Society, gives a graphic description of the lighter side of the peasant's life and of the way in which he amuses himself. There is usually at all their festivals a contest at extempore rhyming between parties of men and women, and, as you may imagine, these contain in good measure vivid allusions to the personal physiognomy and failings of the contestants. Among these he quoted some lines which he heard sung by a girl, and which give a delightful example of Siamese humour. A young man had sung that he came to the girl's front gate and, lover-like, had pleaded for admission. The girl, who did not desire the young man's addresses, sang in reply as follows:—

> "Dai yin si-ang kon ma pon si-ang ma,
> Mai ru cha jā si-ang nai."

To convey the full force of this faithfully in English

is difficult, but the lecturer gives a good idea of the sense in translating it:—

"I heard the voice of a man mingled with the voice of dogs, and I do not know which to respond to."

To picture the scene well, remember that every village house is surrounded by a fence and that pariah dogs are kept inside, which bark at once at the presence or voice of a stranger. The subtle humour, and the insult intended and conveyed in this reply, can only be appreciated to the full by those who know these merry Siamese peasants well.

I have not attempted to cover the whole field of Siamese humour; I have rather tried to point out the kind of humour which appeals to the Siamese mind. Subtleness and wit are of the essence of it, even among the peasant classes, and the example given will be enough, I may hope, to give a glimpse of the humanity of these folk, and to teach us how much akin all peoples are, whether white or brown. As for humour, of a pure unalloyed kind, the story of "The Four Jolly Robbers" can hardly be beaten. The picture of the home-coming villager, who went within the bounds of the sacred thread, being held firmly down on the ground by six strong young men to undergo the pepper cure for his 'madness', must bring a smile to the lips of even the dourest among us.

VII

THE story of "The Glass Stopper" will probably arouse mixed feelings in Western minds. But, even if it is difficult to feel in our hearts any degree of admiration for Kroh Dee, still one cannot help feeling that Phra Chamnān received the exact measure of his deserts. From the moment when he made up his mind to take advantage of the Lao's apparent ignorance and charge him double the amount asked by Kroh Dee for a stone which he himself had declared to be valueless, he was caught in a cleft stick and was doomed. Among the Siamese themselves the laugh would be entirely against Phra Chamnān, and Kroh Dee would be regarded as very 'chalāt'.

This word 'chalāt' may now either mean 'clever' in its natural sense, or it may have the force of 'cunning' or 'crafty'. The use of the word in a bad sense, however, is a recent corruption, and the word 'chalāt' used alone originally meant 'clever', neither more nor less. In order to give it a twisted meaning, it had to be used in conjunction with certain verbs, such as 'len', to play; 'roo', to know; and 'kōng', to deceive.

As, I hope, is clear by now, the Siamese are realists. This is a very wicked world, and everyone is trying to get the better of you in some way or other. Your only means of protection is to be cleverer than your neighbour, and if you can gain a reputation for being alert and keen in your business dealings, you will be looked up to and admired. There is little sympathy wasted on the dupe.

In ordinary social intercourse, except perhaps among very intimate friends, the Siamese employ to a wide extent the art of diplomacy towards one another, and the direct approach would be considered as betraying ignorance, if not a breach of etiquette. This is what makes the Siamese the good diplomats that they unquestionably are. There is a saying which is at times used in speaking of a man, "His tongue is so long that he can wind it round his ears", meaning thereby that he is a very cunning man who can twist his words and so manipulate their use that he can make them mean whatever he pleases. Examples among our own people will no doubt spring to our minds at once. Indeed, the Siamese say themselves that the English language is very elusive, and on this account they hold the English to be very good diplomats. A wise old Siamese statesman, now dead, once remarked that to be a *good* diplomat you must not only be able "to wind your tongue round your ears", but that you must be able to wind it *seven times*!

VIII

THE story which I have called "Celestials in Contrast" is perhaps the most significant and pregnant with meaning for Siam and the Siamese people to-day. Though I am told it is not, it ought to be Chinese in origin, to bring home to the Chinese peasant the urgent need for the homely habit of thrift at the start of his life-journey through the world. Dr. Smiles, had he known this story, would have certainly given it his blessing. But, whatever its source, it applies with rare force to this country to-day, and although these reflections are not intended to be political in character, it must be said that of the two friends who came to seek their fortune in this evergreen and ever-smiling land of plenty, Nguan Heng may well be considered as the prototype of the modern Chinese, and Hah Yong as that of the modern Siamese.

To some European minds it may seem far fetched that a Chinaman can live, as the ordinary indigent Chinaman does, like a cat, upon a daily, monotonous fare of rice and a little salt fish. Not only is this true, but I have heard of cases where the luxury of salt fish has been deliberately foregone, and Chinese coolies working on railway construction have actually seasoned their bowl of rice by cooking the very stones in salt, and then sucking the stones for what nourishment they can extract. This is not getting "blood out of a stone", but it is about as near to it as man will ever get! There is probably no race in the world so imbued with the necessity for hard work and for putting by every cent that remains from the bare cost of keeping their bodies alive. Were they not possessed at the same time with a wild love of gambling in any and every form, they would be the greatest misers that the world has ever seen; but it is curious to see how

Providence redresses the balance in man's nature and does not allow one characteristic to hold full sway over his mind or senses. In the not distant past, the public gambling-houses and lotteries were an important feature of the life of Bangkok, and Chinese could be seen at all hours going to consult the oracle to discover the lucky number for the day. But public gambling is now forbidden by law, and the outlets for indulging in this pastime are necessarily subterranean, so that it is not easy to know to what extent gambling still exists. Yet, even in the old days, the Chinese in Siam never allowed their gambling instinct to override their passion for making money, and by their industry, ability, and honesty they gradually managed to make practically a corner in all the trade of Siam, both internal and external, which was not in the hands of the European or, to a smaller degree, the Indian merchant houses.

The rice-grower has always remained Siamese, and the Chinese have not as yet made any attempt to oust him from that basic position. But the rice-dealer is Chinese. So are the rice-miller and all his coolies. So is the boat-builder, an important handicraft in a country where rivers and canals form the high roads. So are the pawnbroker, the tailor, the boot-maker, the dyer of cloth, the furniture-maker, the iron-smith, the market gardener, the fish-dealer, the old tin-can collector and the hawker. One could go on adding to the list, almost *ad infinitum*, but I have no wish to weary the reader with a recitation of almost every craft known to man. Suffice it to say that, in practically every form of manual labour, the Chinese hold the field, and the Siamese sit by, watching all the requisite services of life being performed by the uniformly impersonal, very vociferous, but intensely industrious Celestial.

Even up to recent years the need to work did not

stand out at all prominently and was not in any way forced upon the attention of the Siamese. All Chinese coming to Siam were treated as Siamese, for as long as they stayed in the country. They intermarried freely with Siamese women, and their children were brought up as loyal Siamese citizens, with little thought of going back to the ancestral home in China.

Twenty years ago you could, figuratively speaking, count the number of Chinese women you saw in Bangkok on the fingers of your two hands. They were, indeed, one of the rarest sights. To-day it is a very different story. The immigration figures for the seven months from December, 1927, to June, 1928, since the Immigration Bureau was established, show that the number of Chinese women and female children who entered and remained in Siam during that period was over twenty thousand. The position has thus radically changed, and for the origin of this change we have not far to seek. The revolution in China in 1911 and the establishment of a Chinese Republic, by introducing and fostering the germ of patriotism and a national spirit, has in the short space of nineteen years already brought about an entirely different outlook in the minds and hearts of the Chinese abroad.

Now the fact that the Chinese immigrants are beginning to bring their wives and families with them to Siam is not, of course, entirely, or even perhaps mainly, due to this spirit of nationalism which has been suddenly developed. Economic causes are probably playing a much greater part, and the scarcity and poverty (which is never far away from the peasants' life in Southern China), caused by the upheaval of all social life in Canton and Swatow, not to speak of the arson, rape, and pillage in which Chinese troops of every brand appear to indulge whenever opportunity offers, is making it almost impossible for Chinese coming to Siam to leave their wives and children behind, as they used to do formerly.

But whatever the cause of their coming, the result is the same. It means that all or most of the Chinese in Siam from henceforward will remain Chinese in thought and spirit. Their children will be taught in Chinese schools, which are springing up all over the country, their wives will talk to them always in Chinese, they will care less and less even to learn Siamese themselves, and they are not likely to be allowed to forget their national spirit or their duties towards their homeland.

Thus in the course of time the Chinese in Siam, of whom there must be at least a million, will assuredly become just as much foreigners as any European race in the country, and those million foreigners will have practically the entire trade of the country in their hands.

IX

TO return now to magic and religion, which after all are the chief burden of these random reflections.

In his discussion in *The Golden Bough* Sir James Frazer makes his own position as clear as possible. After saying that "To frame a definition of religion which would satisfy everyone would obviously be impossible", he gives his own definition, which he employs consistently throughout the work, as follows:—

"By religion, then, I understand 'a propitiation or conciliation of powers superior to man, which are believed to direct and control the course of nature and human life'. Thus defined, religion consists of two elements, a theoretical and a practical, namely, a belief in powers higher than man, and an attempt to propitiate or please them. Of the two, belief clearly comes first, since we must believe in the existence of a divine being before we can attempt to please him. But unless the belief leads to a corresponding practice, it is not a religion but merely a theology; in the language of St. James, 'Faith, if it hath not works, is dead, being alone'."

Sir James then goes on to demonstrate that on the above definition religion is fundamentally opposed to both magic and science, both of which assume that the course of nature is governed, not by the caprices and whims of divine beings, but by the operation of immutable laws acting mechanically, the only difference being that in magic the assumption is implicit, while in science it is explicit, and that magic often deals with 'spirits' which are personal agents of the kind assumed by religion. But, whenever it does so, it treats them exactly in the same way as it treats inanimate agents, that is, it coerces instead of propitiating them as religion would do.

Next, after giving examples of how magic and religion

became confused in the early days, especially in Ancient India and Egypt, he says that "though magic was thus found to amalgamate with religion in many ages and lands, there are grounds for believing that the fusion was not primitive, and that there was a time when man trusted to magic alone to satisfy his other than animal desires. A consideration of the fundamental notions of magic and religion may incline us to surmise that magic is older than religion in the history of humanity, seeing that magic is only a mistaken application of the most elementary processes of the mind, while religion assumes the operation of conscious, personal agents, superior to man, behind the visible screen, obviously a more complex conception".

"If, therefore", he continues, "an Age of Religion has been preceded everywhere by an Age of Magic, we must naturally inquire what causes have led a portion of mankind to abandon magic in favour of religion", and he suggests that the obvious reason lies in the fact that, as man became intelligent, he gradually came to realize the inefficacy of magic to produce the results designed, and this discovery must have wrought a radical though slow revolution in the minds of those who had the sagacity to make it. Having lost one anchorage, mankind must needs seek another, and from a belief in his own power to control nature the deeper mind came to acknowledge powers superior to man, and finally in some cases to absolute dependence on the divine. Sir James adds: "Small minds cannot grasp great ideas: to their narrow vision nothing seems important except themselves. Such minds hardly rise into religion at all. They are indeed drilled by their betters into an outward conformity with its precepts, but at heart they cling to their old magical superstitions, which may be forbidden, but cannot be eradicated by religion."

Having thus dealt with the relationship between magic and religion, and, even in his abridged work, devoted some seven hundred pages to a survey of the magical practices and myths of the world, he concludes his work with the following statement of belief:—

"On consideration of all the circumstances we shall be disposed to conclude that the movement of the higher thought has on the whole been from magic through religion to science. In magic man depends on his own strength to meet the difficulties and dangers that beset him. When he recognized that his control over the forces of nature was purely imaginary, he ceased to rely on his own intelligence, and humbly threw himself on the mercy of certain invisible beings behind the veil of nature, to whom he ascribed all the powers once taken upon himself. Thus magic gave way to religion, but, as time goes on, this explanation in its turn proves to be unsatisfactory. For it assumes that the succession of natural events is not determined by immutable laws, but is variable and irregular, and this assumption is not borne out by closer observation. Thus the keener minds, still pressing forward to a deeper solution of the mysteries of the universe, come to reject the religious theory of nature as inadequate, and revert in a measure to the older standpoint of magic, by postulating explicitly, what in magic was only implicit, an inflexible regularity in the order of natural events, which if carefully observed enables us to foresee their course with certainty and to act accordingly. In short, religion regarded as an explanation of nature is displaced by science. Here, at last, after groping about in the dark for countless ages, man has hit upon a clue to the labyrinth, a golden key that opens many locks in the treasury of nature. It is probably not too much to say that the hope of progress—moral and intellectual as well as material—in the future is bound up with the fortunes of science, and that every obstacle placed in the way of scientific discovery is a wrong to humanity."

Sir James is by no means, however, dogmatic in his claims for science, for he adds that "in the last analysis magic, religion, and science are nothing but theories of thought; and as science has supplanted its predecessors, so it may itself hereafter be superseded by some other more perfect hypothesis, perhaps by some totally different way of looking at the phenomena of which we in this generation can form no idea, for the advance of knowedge is an infinite progression towards a goal that for ever recedes".

I have given what I think to be the substance of Sir James Frazer's views at some little length, because it will be of interest to compare them with the present moral and ethical conditions of Siam at the present time; but before doing so I would like, if with some temerity, to break a friendly lance with Sir James on the general principles underlying his several propositions.

In so far as he holds up before us an Age of Magic as preceding one of Religion, we seem to stand on firm and common ground. It is when he comes to define religion, and to postulate the relation between science and religion, that one feels disposed to part company. As far as it goes, Sir James's definition appears irrefutable, but it by no means goes far enough to satisfy me, the more so when I consider the religion or faith of this country. I would rather take a wider sweep, and define religion as "a conception formed by man of the nature of the Universe of which he is part, of the Power responsible for and governing it, and of his relation towards that Power". This statement contains, I think, all that is implied in Sir James's definition, but it includes much more besides. In his definition Sir James seems to imply something static in the form of religion as adopted by mankind, but, as History teaches us, this is not so, and the definition given above would not in any sense imply such a state; on the contrary, it would make of religion a dynamic force, one of which the conception varied from age to age and among all types of men, according to their stage of development, moral and intellectual. Moreover, it would at once place the relation of science to religion upon an entirely different plane. Sir James writes as if he considers Science an end in itself, but I cannot look upon it as such at all. He speaks of science assuming that the course of nature is governed by the operation of immutable laws acting mechanically. So is the working of an engine. But, even so, no one, scientist or layman, would assume that the engine made itself, or just happened. Somebody must have made the engine, before it could be governed by any laws. In the same way I hold it to be an entirely rational view, from a scientific standpoint, to assume that some Power which, for argument's sake, we will call God, made the Universe before it could be governed by any laws, whether immutable or variable; and that the Power that made the Universe probably made the laws as well. Scientists themselves have to assume hypotheses, and if this view were only acceptable to scientists, it would help to clear the somewhat heated and cloudy atmosphere which still hides religion and science from one another, and raise the work of science, as I have said, to a much more lofty plane without in any way impairing its value. For I hold that science, which seeks for truth in Nature, and religion, which seeks for truth in God, cannot conflict, since Nature is the work of God, and therefore the more we learn of Nature, the nearer we shall approach to God. Science can never be an end in itself—it must be a means to an end, and that the highest one imaginable; and scientists, who kept this end in view and never allowed their work to obscure it from their vision, would not become, as some still do, so lost to the real meaning of life, and so remote from the hearts and yearnings of men. Science is, indeed, the Handmaid of Religion.

I cannot help feeling that the whole difficulty between Science and Religion rests upon the fallacious conception that Religion must necessarily be static. True religion to my mind is nothing of the kind, and one of the greatest stumbling-blocks of this age, this highly intellectual and pragmatic age, is to think that religion still rests either upon forms, or dogmas, or even upon Names and Persons. Buddhism is 2,500 years old; Christianity is 1,900; and Mahommedanism is 1,300. What are these spans of years in the life of man? Gautama, the Buddha, calculated 5,000 years as the limit of duration for his religion. He was wise. There is a popular saying in Siam that at the end of the 5,000 years the Buddhist priest will only have left to him a small piece of yellow cloth resting on his ear!

Who can imagine or conjure up the beliefs of man in another 2,500 years? The fact is that religion was made for man, not man for religion; and that man conceives his form of religion in accordance with his stage of development. It is a common saying that "God made man in His Own Image". A friend of mine once put forward the converse, "Man made God in his own image", as probably more correct, since the idea itself is, must be, entirely man's. But in 2,500 years this Universe will still be here and the Power governing it, and in all probability man will still be here. Let him then, with all reverence, continue to probe the marvellous mysteries before and around him in Nature, and keep steadfastly his own aim in view, to approach nearer to the Power.

And now I come to the second reason why Sir James's definition of religion seems to me inadequate, namely, that, if I accepted it, it would mean that Buddhism is not a religion at all, for it in no way demands a propitiation or conciliation of powers superior to man.

I know it is a popular theory that Buddhism is a system of ethics and not a religion, and colour is lent to this theory by the fact that the Buddha declined to give any explanation of the origin of life or to expound any theory of the Creator of it. But no such teaching as that of Gautama could so have permeated the hearts and minds of the people in such an extensive area of the globe, Ceylon, Java, Burma, Siam, China, and Japan, not to speak of its original home in India, from which it is now cast out; nor endured for such a long period of time without having something more than a system of ethics behind it. Nor would a Buddhist in any of the countries mentioned agree with the popular dictum. In the East it is always called the Buddhist Religion, or the Buddhist Faith, of which, it may be remarked, the King of Siam is now the Head; and I think that, in its widest sense, it does come within the scope of the definition which I have just propounded.

I hope to make this more apparent later on. In the meanwhile, having broken my friendly lance with Sir James Frazer, I would like to make an attempt to apply his propositions to this country, and see how the social, moral, and intellectual conditions of Siam fit in with his general scheme of things.

As will be gathered from the stories you have read, the majority of the people of Siam are still steeped in magic and superstitious beliefs. I need adduce no further proof of this statement here. At the same time, ever since Buddhism was introduced into this country, first in the early centuries of the Christian era by Indian colonists (a number of images of the Buddha of the Gupta period and possibly of earlier schools have been dug up in many parts of the interior in recent years), and again in the seventh and eighth centuries from the Môn kingdom of Lower Burma, magic and superstition have been assailed by an established and orthodox religion. As may be expected, magical practices, which include the exorcising of legions of 'phi' or spirits, are at this time most rife among the Lao in the north and north-east, in the more primitive regions of the Kingdom, and become less and less an outstanding feature of daily life as we come down towards the Capital, Bangkok. The difficulty of eradicating these practices is that, while in theory Buddhism frowns upon them and expressly forbids the worship of spirits as vain, in practice no organized attempt has ever been made by the priests to eradicate them from the minds of the people. Buddhist practice is so tolerant, one might almost say, so easy-going in its attitude towards magic and superstition, that many priests may still be found who, through a desire for popularity or veneration among the people, not only do not discourage superstitious practices, but directly countenance them by blessing amulets and by reciting Buddhist forms of invocation in doing so. It is an interesting and illuminating fact that only recently the Supreme Patriarch of the Kingdom has had to issue an order forbidding Buddhist priests to mix themselves up with anything to do with 'phi' or the occult powers.

The position in Siam is further complicated by the immense influence that the Cambodian Empire has left behind as her contribution to the people of Siam, not only a social influence, but a religious one as well, which in itself was directly borrowed from Brahmin India and which embraced the whole of the Hindu Pantheon. Actually this Cambodian influence, with its belief in gods and guardian angels, helps to fill a gap in the people's minds, although these minds are now very confused as to its significance.

It cannot be said that there is any real conception of God, as the Supreme Creator, in the minds of the Siamese. According to the Siamese idea, this world has no beginning and no ending; but the great Hindu Trinity, Brahma the Creator, Vishnu the Preserver, and Siva the Destroyer, are still known to the people, relics not of their Chinese days but of Cambodian memories, although to the ordinary "man in the street," of whom I write, they are very shadowy figures. There is also another powerful God, much nearer to the Earth, in whom the people generally believe, and that is Indra, who is looked upon as the guardian of the earth and all that is in it.

Indra, whose worship goes back to early Vedic times before the rise of Hinduism in India, and who is the Indian personification of Jupiter (and Thor), plays a very important part in Siam. In Central Siam he is called Phra In, and in Northern Siam Phya In. It may be that Indra is a memory of the earliest days of the Thai race, for he is still known in China, if under a different name. But in any case Indra was a very popular god at the time of the rise of Buddhism, and was adopted by Cambodia along with the Hindu Trinity, when Brahminism with Buddhism came to Angkor Thom. He thus became perpetuated in Siam in later times.

You will very often see in Siamese mural paintings a figure in green representing a Deva, in close proximity to the Buddha. This is Indra, whose duty it is to keep guard and watch over him. Also Indra, who inhabits the Trai Treungsa, the second Heaven, rather near to the earth, is always on the look out to see where trouble is occurring among Kings, Princes, and Peoples in order to be able to put matters right. Some say that he has a soft seat, which suddenly becomes hard; others that his seat is cold, and becomes hot; and there is a stanza from a well-known poem called "Sang Thong", or "the golden conch-shell" of the Second Reign of this Dynasty, which has impressed this belief on the minds of the people:—

> As the god with the thousand eyes
> was musing in the second Heaven,
> the divine throne, which afore was soft,
> became as hard as marble stone;
> and casting his eyes below him
> Indra became alarmed to see
> that somewhere on the throbbing earth
> discord and strife had raised their heads.

This translation is a true one and it conveys the meaning of the passage. Yet, curiously enough, Indra, with all his god-like powers, is regarded as an inferior being altogether to the Buddha, who, although he made no such claim for himself, is looked upon as far superior to all other Beings, whether human or divine.

You will see, then, how all but impossible it is to account for, or to unravel the tangled skein of the ordinary man's beliefs; and yet the reason for such seeming contradiction is not far to seek.

The beliefs of the "man in the street" (whether here or elsewhere) are naturally the outcome of a very slow growth, and are based on long ingrained customs and traditions, handed down and accepted blindly without question. The average man could not coherently account for his beliefs, but in many cases he would fight for them; and I am inclined to think that, in essence, he is fighting not for the beliefs themselves, but to uphold the faith of his fathers and to maintain the *status quo*. Man is at heart intensely conservative.

Yet Buddhism, tolerant as it is, has had a profound influence upon this people, and, to understand in any measure the nature of its influence, we cannot avoid looking somewhat closely at what Buddhism is, its form and substance, and the principles on which it rests. I said in *An Asian Arcady* that to the mass of the people in the north Buddhism represented the "Decoration of Life", while animism was the more domestic article in daily household use. This is to a certain extent true of all Siam, and by the phrase I used I was referring to the numberless rites and ceremonies—all of them of a reverent nature and usually in a beautiful setting—which every Siamese attends throughout his life. But, as with most sayings of this nature, it is not the whole truth, and Buddhism goes far deeper down into the people's lives than mere processions and ceremonies, however solemn and gorgeous, would lead us to believe. So, although I may be expressing what has already been expounded many times before, I would like, without attempting to cover the whole ground, to indicate some idea of the doctrine which Buddhism sets out to teach its adherents.

X

ACCORDING to Rhys Davids, the well-known Pali scholar, the main principle of the Buddha's teaching—one on which he dwelt with peculiar force and emphasis—was the rejection of the Brahminical doctrine of the existence of the individual soul. And here we must remember that Gautama, the Buddha, was of the Kshatriya or Warrior caste, second only to the Brahmin caste itself, and that he must have been imbued from childhood with Brahminical doctrines, which still, even now, in many Buddhist centres, cling to the newer Faith. Put briefly, the main conception of the Universe, as taught by the Brahmins, is one in which Brahma, the Father Almighty, represents the 'Universal Soul', from whom each individual soul emanates, and into which, after all its sailings through calm and tempestuous seas, it will be eventually reabsorbed again.

The pagan teaching of "Eat, drink, and be merry, for to-morrow we die", and the Brahminical teaching of the soul and a life hereafter, both the Buddha held to contain equally false hopes. So he taught the middle path: the impermanence of all things, and the eventual complete dissolution of the being, the escape through Nirvana from all forms of sensation and consciousness which go to make life and suffering; and this by means of the Four Great Truths, which a man must recognize before he sets out on his journey, and the Eightfold Noble Path by which he will attain Nirvana.

And the theory rests upon this. A being is formed of an aggregate of different properties, none of which corresponds to the Christian or Brahmin idea of a 'Soul', namely, twenty-seven Material Attributes, three classes of Feeling, six classes of Perception, fifty-two Elements of Consciousness, and eighty-nine classes of Cognition, together called the Five Skandas, which are developed in the minutest detail in the exposition of the doctrine.

These properties, which are the sum of all the bodily and mental powers and parts of man, are impermanent and constantly changing,[1] and when a being dies, they are dissolved and nothing remains of him. But his 'karma' remains, that is, the aggregate result of all his actions on earth, and as soon as the one being is dissolved, a new sentient being is formed; and this being will enter upon a material state, commensurate with the merit or demerit of the being who has gone.

This doctrine, it must be admitted, rests, as in other religions, not upon any foundation of reason, but on a purely arbitrary notion, beyond the realm almost of speculation, much less of proof.

To make the doctrine still clearer, the theory of the Four Great Truths must be given, and, shortly, it is this:—

(1) All life is suffering;

(2) Suffering is caused by desire (a grasping after material things);

(3) Kill desire, and you kill suffering; by following

(4) The Eightfold Noble Path, and thereby attaining Nirvana.

It may be said in parenthesis that Rhys Davids exposes a fallacy, which has long been abroad, regarding the nature of 'Nirvana'. It does not signify, as so many people suppose, total extinction, for the simple reason that its attainment is reached *on earth*. As soon as one has grasped the Four Great Truths, one enters upon the Eightfold Noble Path of (1) Right Views; (2) Right Aims; (3) Right Words; (4) Right Behaviour; (5) Right Mode of Livelihood; (6) Right Exertion; (7) Right Mindfulness; and (8) Right Meditation; and when a being has reached perfection in all these forms of discipline and control,

[1] We are said to change the tissues of our bodies completely every seven years.

he has attained Nirvana, and is free from Maha-maya, "*the delusion of self*". He is in fact 'enlightened', and has reached a state of blessed peace, above all earthly sensations, desires, sins, and passions. Thus, when such a being dies, all the properties which go to form him are dissolved, and there is no 'karma', no merit or demerit, to hand on to a new sentient being. He has attained Pari-Nirvana, and the aim of his being is achieved. He goes out "like the flame of a lamp".

In connection with the Buddha's teaching, two incidental results of his state of mind should be noticed:—

(1) The abolition of all caste, which naturally gave rise to much discontent; and

(2) Contempt for all ritual, rites, and ceremonies.

The question of caste was probably one of the chief ultimate causes of the exclusion of Buddhism from India, since it touched the Brahmin in his weakest spot; but obviously, from Gautama's point of view, if it was possible for any being to attain Nirvana, such a system as Caste was impossible. Also, if everything on earth was involved in Maya, or delusion, of what possible value were rites and ceremonies?

The ethics of Buddhism show but little difference from those of Christianity, and what differences there may be are due in the main to different conditions of life. Here are the first five Commandments:—

(1) Do not kill.

(2) Do not steal.

(3) Do not bear false witness.

(4) Do not commit adultery.

(5) Do not drink intoxicating liquor.

This last commandment is only binding on priests, and not, as in Mohammedanism, on all. From the ethical point of view, these are surely the most binding Commandments on every Christian, too, in the conduct of his daily life.

The attractiveness of the Buddhist doctrine, as Rhys Davids says, and as will be seen from the story, "The Keeper of the Book", lies in the idea of 'karma', which represents for each one of us a kind of balance-sheet, and therein lies one of its fundamental differences from Christianity. Christ taught the existence of God the Father, the Creator of the world, and through redemption by His own sacrifice held out a hope of immortal life for the soul of each individual man. But Buddha gave no account of the creation of the world or life, and God is conceived, if at all, in terms of mind, not matter (i.e. not as a Being). He accepted life as he found it, and taught the non-existence of the soul, and the Way of Escape from an impermanent, sorrowful life.

I have given above what I understand to be the fundamental doctrines of Buddhism as expounded by a great scholar. In the nineteenth century there seem, however, to have been ideas abroad in Europe that the soul of man was involved in the teaching. Amiel, for instance, who toys a good deal with Buddhism in his *Journal Intime*, appears to think that the devout Buddhist is eagerly looking forward to the 'dissolution' or 'annihilation' of the soul itself. And I myself must confess that I have often wondered whether Gautama's teaching has been misunderstood, or, if that is not possible and it is certain that the denial of a soul was part of the original teaching, whether this teaching has been able to survive the test of 2,500 years.

In Siam, at least, the Buddhist doctrine as taught by the Thammayut Sect[1] does not exclude the idea of a soul in man, and in fact teaches the transmigration of souls. By this teaching I mean that the same 'ego' or conscious personality of a being goes from life to life,

[1] There are two Buddhist sects in Siam, the Mahanikai and the Thammayut. The former is by far the more numerous.

on a higher or lower plane according to the nature of his 'karma', and that this personality does not become extinct with the death of a being. It is easy to understand why the doctrine of soul-negation finds it difficult to survive. It is far too abstract a theme for ordinary mortals to grasp; it could only be addressed to a highly developed and intellectual society. For it means that you must embrace the Four Great Truths and follow the Eightfold Noble Path for their own sakes, and not because of any reward or punishment that you may receive hereafter in another life. You live and act worthily during this life so that, although you yourself are removed for ever from the stage, the impression, the remembrance, the example of your high moral standards may remain as a definite and permanent influence upon those that come after. But this is too much to ask, and so, in all human relations, whether of a religious nature or not, the average human being must be offered a certain reward for being a 'good boy', and threatened with dire consequences for being a 'bad boy', in this life. It is the old picture of Heaven and Hell—rewards and punishments—from which our teachers never seem to be able to rid themselves in their desire to make us good. We are all children, very young children, and fear is still, it seems, the only stimulus to our better nature; a sugar-plum if we behave ourselves well, but a big stick if we are naughty.

Yet there is no gainsaying the implied aim of the Eightfold Noble Path to perfect oneself in this life, in the same way as Christ taught his world to aim at perfection, "Be ye perfect, even as your Father in Heaven is perfect." It is true that Gautama taught renunciation, self-denial, withdrawal from the world, in short, the monastic life, as the surest means of overcoming sin and sorrow, and of escaping from the relentless wheel of life; whereas Christ taught a life of action and service to one's fellow-men as a means of perfection. But the word 'perfect' itself is only another word for 'divine', and one cannot escape the feeling that the end of a life spent in attaining Nirvana through the agency of the Eightfold Noble Path would be a state of Perfect Blessedness, where the being became one with the source from which he came, and was absorbed back into the Universal Soul, as taught by the Brahmins.

Havell, in his *Indian Art*, seems to give expression to a somewhat similar thought when he speaks of the Buddha, having attained Maha Pari Nirvana at death, passing into the boundless Ocean of Eternity, and reaching a state of Perfect Blessedness, free for ever from the sufferings of the body and the great illusion of the senses, the Maha-Maya.

There is, I believe, among scientists at home to-day, and among their disciples, a considerable school of materialists who are seeking to reduce, and believe they can succeed in reducing, everything in life and nature to a question of physics, and who thus strenuously oppose the idea of an immaterial, intangible soul in man.

It is a bold school, and one which is sure to attract a number of adherents; but even if life and nature could be dissected like an insect into all its component parts and atoms (as I daresay it will be), what then? The dissectors would be no nearer to their proof that there was no soul, but would only demonstrate that they in their turn had missed it. No dissection of my physical properties will ever give an adequate explanation of why I am urged to write as I do, or why I see beauty in a rainbow-crowned sky. I cannot explain it to myself, but I feel and I know that some active personal agent prompts me to do so, and the measure of my words or of my sense of beauty will be governed by the state of development of my soul, how far I can peer into the dim hall of Truth, or what glimpse I can catch of the Goddess Beauty enthroned on high.

Indeed, we Europeans are becoming altogether too sophisticated. Scientists, grave, practical men of fixed aims, have no compunction nowadays in tearing all our romances to shreds, and in leaving us nothing but the bare facts of life, as they see them, on which to feed. Yet, if they only knew, they might deal more kindly with us, for at present the capacity of the highest human intellect is still infinitesimally small, and the truths the learned ones find are only relative after all. May it not be that millenniums to come will marvel at the abysmal ignorance of this age, and be faintly amused at our dogmatic assertions of the 'truth'?

This is why it always gives me joy to turn, whenever I can, from this matter-of-fact world and from the icy land of science and wander among the warm life-giving airs of fairyland, to feel the pulse quicken and the spirit enriched by a thousand echoes, memories, and voices which come and go, borne on fairy wings, conjuring up the past, and sometimes even giving, perhaps, shadowy glimpses of the future. As long as a fairy-tale remains, I will never agree to Man being reduced to a question of physics, to a conglomeration of formulæ. The inflexible scientist will warn me that, whether I oppose him or not, I cannot escape the inevitable conclusion of his relentless hunt; but I snap my fingers at him, for I know that we are "such stuff as dreams are made on", and that there is in Man something which will always elude the wretch's grasp, however hard he may search. At the last I can always hide in fairyland, where no man of science is allowed to enter, and where I can spend my time in capturing gossamer threads and dreams. But to do this I must throw off my matter-of-fact, everyday dress, and clothe myself in imagination's garb, or I shall never be allowed to enter the gate.

XI

SOME years ago an economic inquiry was set on foot in a district in North-Eastern Siam which yielded interesting results.

From this particular district there is every year a migration of peasants to the padi plains in the Circle of Ayudhya, which is the principal rice-producing district of Siam. These peasants come for the padi season, ploughing, sowing, and reaping, which lasts six months, and receive in return free board and lodging and a sum of about seven or eight pounds from the farmer who hires them. As soon as the padi is reaped, they return to their homes. Now it has been found that this sum, seven or eight pounds, is enough actual money to last the peasant and his family for three years! This works out at about four shillings a month, but it is enough to buy salt and perhaps matches, which are all he requires.

In the country where he lives he can go out into the jungle near by and cut his own bamboo to build his house and fences. Rice-seed is obtainable at all times for nothing, and he can grow his own little patch of padi. Tobacco, too, is almost wild, and this he cultivates as well. His women-folk keep silkworms and weave their own skirts, while the cotton-tree gives him all the thread he requires. There are fish in the stream at hand, and a dozen fowls roost and lay their eggs beneath his house. What more does he require to buy? Am I not right in calling parts of this land a real Asian Arcady? These people, too, if primitive in their thoughts and outlook, have a pretty high standard of morals among themselves, and there are still villages in Siam where sexual diseases are unknown, and from which an offender has been incontinently expelled.

Another example of the value of money in the up-country districts was given me by a Siamese official a short time ago. He was visiting friends in the north, and one day went out into a village and began conversing with some of the old men whom he met. Finding him of a friendly disposition, they asked him all sorts of questions, how many wives and families he had, what his clothes cost, and finally what was the amount of his salary. Now the official in question was drawing about 400 ticals (say £40) a month, but he knew it would be no use for him to say so; they simply would not believe him. So he answered with a smile, "Oh, twenty ticals a month." Whereupon, even to his own astonishment, one of the old men looked at him with shining eyes and said, "What do you do with it all?" And further inquiries on the official's part elicited the fact that the questioner was pretty well content with four ticals a month, and that twenty ticals seemed to him to betoken the wealth of Crœsus.

Reference to the arcadian conditions of life in some parts of this country recalls the pictures shown in the famous film 'Chang', which presents this life to the full. You can see for yourselves how 'Kru', the hunter, built his home, tilled his little field of rice, and hunted his game, while his wife attended, not to the luxuries, but to the necessities of housekeeping. That picture, except of course for the amount of wild animal life surrounding him, does not exaggerate 'Kru's' mode of living. 'Chang' is, indeed, a magnificent picture, and the sight of the leopard scaling the twelve-foot palisade, as a cat would softly leap on to a table, without any preliminary take-off or spring, will never cease to rouse in me a feeling of wonder at the enormous power in their haunches.

The thought of 'Kru' and his jungle life reminds me

of an incident which happened some years ago in Pitsanulok, and which brought me into contact with the Siamese peasant-hunter in a very entertaining manner. I was staying in Pitsanulok on business, and one evening took a walk along the river bank. After going some distance I came upon a party of Siamese peasants squatting in a 'Sala', or open rest-house, near the road. Some of them had guns, some of them had baskets, and they all seemed weary, as if they had travelled a long distance. So I went up to an elderly man, who appeared to be the leader of the band, and asked him where they came from and where they were going. He told me that he and his friends, having raised between them the sum of five hundred ticals, had left Petchabūn, a small town in the heart of Siam about seventy miles south-east of Pitsanulok, in the month of February, and had gone north to the Chieng Rai district, over 250 miles away, in search of rhinoceros. They were now, in the month of June, having used up all their money, returning to their homes empty handed after four months' fruitless search. Knowing the Chieng Rai district to teem with game of every kind, I was a little surprised at this, and expressed my astonishment at their not having tried to obtain a 'bag' of tiger, leopard, sambhur, and wild pig, which would at least have given them something to bring home and have recompensed them for their time and trouble. The old man looked at me for a moment, and then naturally and directly replied, "We were not after small game!" It made me smile to wonder how many of our big shikaris would regard tiger and leopard as 'small game'; but it is probably because these people, so to speak, live with the feline tribe all around them that they come to regard them without much feeling of awe. Certainly the two-horned rhinoceros, which is becoming exceedingly scarce in Siam now, is a very attractive 'bag'. Every scrap of it is used for some purpose or other, from its hide to its teeth and its horn, and I have heard the carcase valued at as much as 2,000 ticals (nearly £200). Much of it is used in preparing medicines, and parts of it, the horn at least, possess prodigious power and efficacy as charms.

Now, although such a family as I have depicted above must needs live a pretty active, wary life, it is not one which is likely to lead to great exertions on behalf of others. Indeed, their very activity is a kind of negative activity, their whole lives being spent in housing, feeding, and clothing themselves, and in conciliating and warding off the 'spirits' that encompass them.

And yet to all these folk Buddhism is a real thing. Wherever there is a village you will find a temple not far off, with the image of the Buddha sitting in serene contemplation on the altar. It may be an elaborate brick structure with white-washed walls set in a garden of leafy trees, fig and tamarind; or it may be formed of pillars supporting a shingle roof without walls at all; or it may be just a wooden shanty with an attap roof and a mud floor. Still, it is their temple all the same, and there they will be found at all times paying their devotions to the greatest Being they know. There are computed to be over seventeen thousand temples actually in use in this land, excluding those of ancient days that have fallen to ruin, and this is one to every six hundred people, a brave average for folk who are not in any way blessed with the riches of this world. In all probability the humble peasant has no idea whether he possesses a soul or not, and would scarcely understand you if you asked him. But they all know the doctrine of 'karma', and that, if they do not wish to be born again as a serpent or a rat, they must take care that they leave a balance on the credit side of their account. So you can understand how Buddhism is peculiarly suited to this and other Far Eastern lands, with its calm and peaceful meditation through the heat of the tropic day.

I wonder sometimes whether it is fully realized how much the choice of a religion by a nation is due to its climatic as well as to its social conditions. How easy it is to see that Buddhism can make but little appeal in a northern clime, where untiring energy and ceaseless activity is necessary to maintain our vitality and keep our blood from congealing in our bodies, to say nothing of earning our living. Calm contemplation in Greenwich Park throughout the winter would hardly conduce to a subdual of the bodily passions, or to freedom from the illusion of self, except in the form of voluntary suicide.

But these primitive, arcadian conditions in Siam are going to change, and with them the lives of the people. The railway is forging rapidly ahead, and with it will go many of the accompaniments of our modern Western civilization. Roads are springing up on all sides, and hundreds of Ford and Chevrolet cars and trucks are pouring into the country to serve the up-country districts. The cinema hall, put up in a day with tin roof and bamboo sides, is early in the field, and cheap American cigarettes soon begin to oust the native-made tobacco. Townlets arise, seemingly from nowhere as in the pantomime, conjured up out of the brain of the ubiquitous Chinaman, who is prepared to buy and sell anything that will bring grist to his mill. What of my arcadian peasant, after a few years' mingling with all the rogues and vagrants of the place, irresistibly drawn by the thought of sheep to be fleeced? I have heard it said already that when the emigrants now return yearly from their work in the Ayudhya plains, they have to be guarded to their homes by the gendarmerie, or they would lose their little all at the hands of the pack of wolves that stand hungrily round the station of Korat with protruding tongues, waiting for the sheep to arrive.

We cannot stop the march of progress if we would. The world is growing smaller and smaller every year, and scarcely any action of importance can take place nowadays in one country without its echoes reverberating throughout the others in a short space of time. But although you can within a few years develop a country materially by introducing all the most modern inventions, you cannot automatically, by pressing a button, develop the moral and spiritual nature of the people of that country, to enable them to appraise these material changes at their proper value. You and I know how much more real pleasure is to be obtained from a walk through beautiful surroundings, costing nothing but the effort, than from the most lavish theatrical or cinematograph display. But how are they to know it? Still the future must be faced with confidence, and the present looked upon as a transitional period from which the people will in time emerge with a higher standard of living and better equipped to maintain themselves against all comers.